GODBODY

GODBODY

by THEODORE STURGEON

DONALD I. FINE, INC.
New York

AGAPE AND EROS: THE ART OF THEODORE STURGEON

BY ROBERT A. HEINLEIN

GODBODY—
"The Last of the Wine."
And the best.

Sometimes (not often) the last work of an artist, published after his death, is the capstone of his art, summing up what he had been telling the world all his life. In writing *Godbody* Theodore Sturgeon achieved this crowning statement. Again and again for half a century he has given us one message. In *Godbody* he tells us still again, and even more emphatically, the same timeless message that runs through all his writings and through all his living acts—a message that was ancient before he was born but which he made his own, then spoke it and sang it and shouted it and sometimes scolded us with it:

"Love one another."
Simple. Ancient. Difficult.
Seldom attained.

Early this century, before World War I, I was taught in Sunday school that Jesus loves us, you and me and everyone, saint and sinner alike. Then the Kaiser raped poor innocent Belgium, and never again did the world seem sweet and warm and safe. Today I cannot promise you that Jesus loves you, but I can assure you that Ted Sturgeon loves you . . . did love you and does today—"does," present tense, because what I still hold of my childhood faith includes a conviction that Ted did not cease to be when his worn-out body stopped breathing. It may be that villains die utterly. But not saints.

In fifty years of storytelling Sturgeon spoke to us of love, again and again and yet again, without ever repeating himself. One of the marks of his art was his unique talent for looking at an old situation from a new angle, one that no one else had ever noticed. He did not imitate (and could not be imitated) . . . and each of his stories was a love story.

Examples:

"Bianca's Hands." (That one? A story so horrible that editors not only bounced it but blacklisted the author? Yes, that one.)

"The World Well Lost." (A love story, obviously—one about homosexuals. But please note that the copyright on it is 1953, many years before "gay pride" was even whispered, much less shouted. And Ted was not speaking in defense of himself but out of empathy for others. Ted was not even mildly homosexual. You can check this for yourself if you wish. I have no need to; I knew him intimately for more than forty years.)

"Some of Your Blood." (Go back and read it again. Yes, George Smith makes Count Dracula look like a tenderfoot Scout. But Sturgeon invites you to look at it from George Smith's angle.)

And so on, story after story for half a century. Some of Sturgeon's yarns had adventure trappings, or science-fiction gadgets, or fantasy/weird/horror props, or whodunnit gimmicks or other McGuffins, but in each, tucked away or displayed openly, you will find some searching comment on love, a new statement, not something borrowed from another writer.

In addition to this prime interest Ted was alive to every facet of the world around him: He had a lifelong passion for machinery; his interest in music was intense and professional; he delighted in travel; he relished teaching others what he had learned—but above all and at all times, waking and sleeping, he loved his fellow humans and expressed it in all aspects of his life.

I first met Theodore Sturgeon in 1944. He had just returned from the Caribbean, where he had been a heavy-machinery operator building airstrips for the U.S. Army Air Force. That job played out in '44; no more airfields were being built in the Antilles; the emphasis was shifting to the Pacific Theater. Ted was 4-F, a waste of skin; his draft board laughed at him. He was not even eligible for limited service. Rheumatic fever in his high-school days had left him with a heart so disabled that simply staying alive through each day was a separate miracle.

That damaged heart not only kept Ted out of military service; ten years earlier it had robbed him of his dearest ambition: to be a circus acrobat. In high school, by grueling daily practice, he had transformed himself from that fabled ninety-pound weakling into a heavily muscled and highly skilled tumbler, one who could reasonably hope to join someday the "Greatest Show on Earth." Then one morning he woke up ill.

He recovered . . . but with a badly damaged heart. A circus career was out of the question, and many other pursuits were foreclosed. Eventually his disability forced him into the one career open to anyone whose body is warm and mind still functioning: free-lance writing.

I once collected notes for an essay—the relation between

physical disability and the literary pursuit; or Shakespeare
was 4-F and so was Lord Byron and Julius Caesar and
Somerset Maugham—and what's your excuse, brother?
Was it a queasy itch to see your name in print and a distaste
for hard work? Or was it diabetes (polio, consumption,
heart trouble) and a pressing need to pay the rent?

If we limit the discussion to science fiction, I can recall
offhand several writers who got into the business not from
choice but from physical disability coupled with financial
necessity: Theodore Sturgeon, Robert A. Heinlein, Cleve
Cartmill, H. G. Wells, Fletcher Pratt, Daniel F. Galouye, J.
T. McIntosh. Each on this list wound up as a free-lance
writer through physical limitations that crowded him into
it . . . and I am sure that the list could be much longer, if
we but knew.

So what was Sturgeon doing running bulldozers and
backhoes and power shovels? Driving a Daisy Eight is not
as easy as driving a car; rassling a dozer is no job for a man
with a bad heart.

The answer is simple: Ted never paid any more attention
to his physical limitations than he was forced to, and in
wartime the physical examination for a civilian employee of
the army or navy consisted of walking past the surgeon,
who would then mark the prospect "fit for heavy manual
labor." I am not joking. In World War II, I hired many
civilians for the Navy Field Service; the Army Field Service
was not more demanding than we were—or we would have
snatched their prospects away from them. This was a time
when any warm body would do. A typist was a girl who
could tell a typewriter from a washing machine. (Later we
took out the washing machine.)

So Ted built airstrips in broiling sun and 120-degree
heat and failed to drop dead. He outlasted the job and then
came to New York.

I think Ted worked for a while for the University of California, in the Empire State Building, with John W. Campbell, Jr., the editor of *Astounding Science Fiction,* as his supervisor. No, I have not jumped my trolley; at that time the University of California occupied one entire floor in the Empire State Building. Campbell was supervisor in a classified section that wrote radar operation and maintenance manuals—and even the word "radar" was classified; one did not say that word. (And didn't even *think* the word "uranium," not even in one's sleep.)

I am not certain what work Ted did, because in 1944 one did not poke into another man's classified work. I knew a trifle about this radar project because I had a radar project of my own, with a touch of overlap. But Campbell is dead now, and so is George O. Smith and so is Ted; I can't check. (Ted's wife Jayne can't be certain; I am speaking of the year she was born.)

As may be, Ted was writing at night for Campbell and sharing lodging with Jay Stanton, who was both Campbell's assistant supervisor on the radar writing project and Campbell's assistant editor at Street and Smith . . . and all three men were part of another project I ran for OpNav-23, a brainstorming job on antikamikaze measures. (I was wearing three hats, not unusual then. One tended to live on aspirin and soothing syrup.)

I had been ordered to round up science-fiction writers for this crash project—the wildest brains I could find, so Ted was a welcome recruit. Some of the others were George O. Smith, John W. Campbell, Jr., Murray Leinster, L. Ron Hubbard, Sprague de Camp, and Fletcher Pratt. On Saturday nights and Sundays this group usually gathered at my apartment in downtown Philadelphia.

At my request Campbell brought Sturgeon there. My first impression of Sturgeon was that no male had any business being that pretty. He was a golden boy, one that caused comparisons with Michelangelo's David. Or Baldur. He was twenty-six but looked about twenty. He was tall, straight, broad-shouldered, and carried himself with the grace of a tightwire artist. He had a crown of golden curls, classic features and a sweet, permanent smile.

All this would have been inexcusable had it not been that he was honestly humble and warmly charming. When others spoke, Sturgeon listened with full attention. His interest in others caused one to forget his physical beauty.

My flat was about three hundred yards from the Broad Street Station; people came to these meetings from Washington, Scarsdale, Princeton, the Main Line, Manhattan, Arlington, etc.; my place was the most convenient rendezvous for most of the group. No one could drive a car (war restrictions), but the trains every thirty minutes on the Pennsylvania Railroad could get any member of the group there in two hours or less. It was a good neutral ground, too, for meetings that might include several officers (lieutenant to admiral), a corporal from OSS, a State Department officer, one sergeant, civil servants ranging from P-1 to P-6, contractors' employees with clearances up to "top secret" but limited by "need to know," and civilians with no official status and no clearance. I never worried about security because there was always one member of naval intelligence invariably present.

On Saturday nights there would be two or three in my bed, a couple on the couch and the rest on the living-room floor. If there was still overflow, I sent them a block down the street to a friend with more floor space if not beds. Hotel rooms? Let's not be silly; this was 1944.

The first weekend Sturgeon was there he slept on the hall rug, a choice spot, while both L. Ron Hubbard and George O. Smith were in the overflow who had to walk down the street. In retrospect that seems like a wrong decision; Hubbard should not have been asked to walk, as both of his feet had been broken (drumhead-type injury) when his last ship was bombed. Ron had had a busy war—sunk four times and wounded again and again—and at that time was on limited duty at Princeton, attending military governors' school.

On Sunday afternoon the working meeting was over, and we were sitting around in my living room. Ron and Ted had been swapping stories and horrible puns and harmonizing on songs—both were fine vocalists, one baritone, one tenor. I think it was the first time they had met, and they obviously enjoyed each other's company.

Ron had run through a burlesque skit, playing all the parts; then Ted got up and made a speech "explaining" Marxism and featuring puns such as "Engels with dirty faces" (groan), and ending with "then comes the Revolution!" At that last word he jumped straight up into the air and into a full revolution—a back flip. His heels missed the ceiling by a scant inch, and he landed as perfectly as Mary Lou Retton on the exact spot on which he had been standing.

This with no warning—which is how I learned that Ted was a tumbler. This in a crowded room. This with no wind-up. I don't think he could have done it in a phone booth but he did not have much more room.

Ron Hubbard leaned toward me, said quietly into my ear, "Uh huh, I can see him now, a skinny kid in a clown suit too big for him, piling out of that little car with the other clowns and bouncing straight into his routine."

Ron was almost right.

I think it was a later weekend that we learned of Ted's incredible ability to produce just from his vocal cords, no props, any sound he had ever heard—traffic noises, train noises, shipboard noises, animals, birds, machinery, any accent whatever.

Here is the first one I asked for: A frosty morning, a

buzzsaw powered by a two-cycle engine cranked by a line. Start the engine despite the freezing weather, then use the saw to cut firewood. The saw hits a nail in the wood.

I'm sorry I can't offer you a tape. Ted scored a cold four-oh.

Thirty-three years later, in front of a large audience at San Diego ComiCon, I asked Sturgeon to repeat that buzz-saw routine, defining it again for him, as he had forgotten ever doing it. He thought for a few seconds, then did it. Another four-oh.

The second one I demanded was this: A hen lays an egg, then announces it. The farm wife shoos her off the nest long enough to grab the egg and replace it with a china egg.

Another perfect score—I do not know when or where Sturgeon coped with cranky two-cycle engines or with temperamental hens . . . but this farm boy now speaking can testify that Ted had been there in each case and could reproduce the sounds as exactly as any equipment from Sony or Mitsubishi.

I hope that someone somewhere has taped and preserved some of Sturgeon's jokes in dialect. I would like to hear again the one about the pub in London where one could get a bit of bread, a bit of cheese, a pint of bitter, a gammon of Yorkshire ham, a bit of pudding and a go with the barmaid, all for two and six. Try to imagine all *that.* Was anyone running a recorder?

Ted's ear was phenomenal and not limited to parlor tricks. Mark Twain said that the difference between the right word and almost the right word was the difference between lightning and a lightning bug.

Sturgeon did not deal in lightning bugs.

Exempli gratia:

Godbody is written in multiple first person, a difficult narrative technique, believe me. Try this experiment. After you read *Godbody,* open it up anywhere, read three lines. Note the page number and write down who, in your opinion, is speaking. Do this several times.

Better yet, have someone help you, so that you do not know where the sample comes from—beginning, middle or end.

I predict that you will call correctly which of eight characters spoke each of these small samples.

Yet Sturgeon makes almost no use of spelled-out eccentricities of speech or other flags to mark his characters. Flagging is mechanical, a device any hack writer can copy. What Sturgeon does is subtle—each character has his own voice. How do you know at once who is calling on the telephone, if the caller is one familiar to you? By the caller's voice, of course.

How does Sturgeon do this? First let's dissect Paderewski's hands to learn how he played the piano; then we'll dissect Sturgeon's brain to learn how he could give an imaginary person his own unique voice. Art on this level resists analysis; the critic who tries it gets egg on his face.

Godbody—Forget about art and enjoy it.

Some readers will feel that it is XXX-rated pornography. They will have plenty to go on.

Others will see it as a tender, gentle love story. They'll be right.

Many will find it offensively coarse in language (people of my generation, especially). It does contain every one of the "seven words that must never be used on television," plus four or five more that can't be used but never got on the verboten list.

Others will see that Ted has always used the exact word —always "lightning," never "lightning bug." Those four-letter shockers are essential.

Some will complain that *Godbody* is loaded with sex and violence.

Others may answer that "Hamlet" ("Romeo and Juliet," the Old Testament, *Le Morte d'Arthur*) is nothing but sex and violence.

Some will denounce *Godbody* as baldly sacrilegious. They'll be right.

Others will see it as tenderly and beautifully reverent. And they will be right.

Others will say, "Yes, it's a great story. But why did he have to stick so much nudity into it?"

I'll answer that one myself, since it is too late to ask Sturgeon. God must love skin since he makes so much of it. Covering it with cloth or leather or fur in the name of "decency" is a vice thought up by dirty old men; don't blame it on God.

Never mind what anyone says about this book. Read it, enjoy it, reread it, give it to someone you love. It is our last love letter from a man who loves all of us. Make the most of it today. Then keep it for a day when you are down-hearted and need what it gives you.

And don't be afraid to love.

—R.A.H, September, 1985

Dan Currier

IT MAY BE THAT after all this time, and after all that has happened, I do not remember that first time as it really was. Perhaps I remember it as it should have been; we do that sometimes, all of us. Whatever I've added, if I've added anything, was the right touch; the memory is perfect:

Midmorning, late spring in the Catskills, and the mist burning away, but still there an underwater-green with the rich new greenness of the spring-struck trees radiating through it. A broken old stone fence, green-grey, and at the corner of the two roads, he sat naked. He alone in all that green universe was red, was reds: fine hair down to his earlobes copper-orange, slab-sided cheeks picking a ripe-peach-red out of the bars of sun, gold-red on the down of his chest and lower belly. He was sitting absolutely bone-less, comfortably round-shouldered, and with his chin gone to bed on his collarbones.

And—maybe this is the part I've added, but it remembers like a real memory, and I'd like to think it happened that way—around his head flew a circle of white moths, turned pale, pale apple-green in that light and amazing against that hair. I stopped the car. I don't think it was because he was naked.

Because I couldn't help myself, I called to him, "Hey!"

He raised his head, swiftly but not startled, and opened his eyes; then, as part of a flowing sequence without stopping anywhere, he placed his hands on the stones and lifted himself and vaulted down, landing lightly and already walking. Walking, his body moved forward as if on tracks, not bobbing up and down the way most of the rest of us do. If his shoulders had been the least bit wider they would have been too wide; if his body were by a finger's breadth flatter it would have been too flat. He made no attempt to cover his nakedness and he wasn't displaying it, either; it just didn't matter to him. The moths whisked away in the wood as he stepped out in the road.

Then: his eyes. Think back now; in all the talk, in everything you have read or heard about Godbody, has anyone ever used a color-word for Godbody's eyes? Someone with hair that color is called a redhead, but redheads don't have red hair; it's orange or russet or brown-gold, and you just can't say that this man had red eyes and be right. Cinnamon, maybe, but that's too brown. Sherry is too yellow, ruby is too red. His eyes were a rich color, that's all you can say, and warm. He bent to put his elbows on the edge of the open window of the car and looked in at me and smiled. "Hi."

What do you say? I didn't know. I tried this: "What you doing, man?"

He took it as a straight question and gave me what was for him a straight answer. "Bein' a bird."

"What?"

Now you have to believe me: what came next was said with no effort to make impressions, or to startle. It was only the truth—his truth. "Was a bird for about an hour," he said. "Tell you something about birds. People go around all the time sayin', 'Am I a man? Am I a woman, a real woman?' Lookin' at what they've done, wonderin' if that's what a man would do. Now, birds: they just birds. The one thing they *never* do is say, 'Am I a bird?' "

I laughed. I'm afraid it was a silly little bleat of a laugh, but what do you say? Now I tried this: "What's your name?"

"Godbody."

"My name's Currier."

He just hung there on the window for the longest time without speaking. I kept looking at him because in some peculiar way I was afraid not to. I began to feel that I had to move, so I moved my feet; to turn my head would have broken something, and that would have been pretty bad. You don't know what I mean. Neither did I at the time; neither do I now.

At last he touched me. He put his right hand very firmly just where my neck meets my shoulder. He had to slide his hand part way under my sports shirt to do it. My reaction was violent but motionless: does that say anything? The contact evoked a wild desire to do something, and a jaw-bunched, tooth-gritting effort not to. They canceled out, and it cost. Then he took his hand away.

"Why did you do that?"

In that straight-answer way of his, he said, " 'Currier' don't say anything. I wanted to find out who you are."

Again (annoying myself) I produced that stupid bleat. "Who am I, then?"

He straightened up and smiled. "I'll be seeing *you* again," he said, and turned and sprang across the ditch and up onto the old wall. He waved once and dropped down out of sight into the dim green of the wood.

I sat there for some time like a stopped clock; nothing seemed to be happening inside at all. Perhaps the whole thing was soaking in, slowly. Then I found myself looking at the corner of the wall where I had first seen him, with a momentary feeling of disbelief. I actually craned my head out of the car window to see if he had left any footprints. Then there were his words, especially the last ones; the little emphasis he put on one word changed a rubber-stamp phrase like "I'll be seeing you again" into a message.

Then there was that hand on my shoulder. I sat there trying to resist the temptation to reach up there and touch the place, for I could feel that electric contact just as if the hand were still there. I was trying to resist, I found, because to do so might wipe it away. I should have known better. It is there to this day. And this resistance brought to mind that other, the thing I wanted so desperately to do when he touched me. All I knew then was that it cost, it cost terribly not to do the thing I wanted to do, but I didn't know what it was. I know now.

In short—I was very upset. I started the car and turned it around. I had things to do, people to see, but all I wanted then was home, and Liza. Driving back down the twisting dirt road to the highway, and then through town, I looked more or less as usual to people I passed, I suppose; I have a vague recollection of waving to one and smiling at another; but somehow I knew that there was in me an irreversible change, and all I could do, over and over again, was to ask myself the special question I used to guide me in my calling, and by which I judged all my decisions: "I am ordained a man of God; what has this to do with how I am behaving?" There was no answer, no matter how often or how intensely I asked; home and Liza, Liza and home were all that could matter.

The rest I remember less clearly, but more real; I mean, it doesn't have the crystal perfection in my mind that gives my first glimpse of Godbody that dreamlike quality. I pulled into the drive and all the way to the garage doors, so I could go in the back, and went in through the kitchen. There was a flash of annoyance when I heard a man's voice —only because of the pressure of wanting to be with Liza alone. It was Wellen—"Hobo" Wellen they called him, because his name was Hobart, and certainly not because of anything else about him. Hobo was one of those people who look tailored even in store-bought jeans, whose teeth are straighter than they ought to be and whose hair always seems to be blown exactly into place by any passing wind. People like that always make me feel too big and clumsy and put-together wrong, and somehow seem to have easy answers to things which puzzle me all the time.

"Hi, Rev," he said with that bright smile of his. "Just dropped by to tell you a funny, and found you gone and a damsel in distress."

"Oh darling, I'm glad you're back." Liza was pink and happy-looking. The drapes were down from the north windows and lying over the trestle table. "I just washed the windows and Hobo was trying to help me put the drapes back up."

"Well, thanks, Hobo," I said.

"It was nothing," Hobo said. "It really was nothing—I couldn't do it. I'll leave it to you—you can go down on your knees and still reach up there."

One thing I had learned about Hobo Wellen—never that I can recall, not once, did he speak to me without at least one reference to my size. He always made me feel that I had done something ridiculous to grow to six-four and that I should have known better. I said, "I appreciate it anyway, Hobo."

"I'll give you the funny," Hobo said, "and then I got to cut out." This was one of Hobo's pastimes; I can't say I enjoyed it but it apparently did him some good, and it was harmless, although sometimes his 'funnies' weren't funny, and sometimes I wished he wouldn't tell them in front of Liza. When you're a minister you go along with things, though. They say of some pastors and priests, "He'll take a drink, tell a yarn along with the rest of us," and this is supposed to make them better at their jobs. I don't do either one, but I find myself listening all the same, even at times like this, when I wanted desperately to be doing something else. This time the funny was about an airplane and the captain's voice announcing that three of the engines had failed and the plane would crash. Instant panic, and then someone cried out "Somebody do something religious!" whereupon a gentleman in the front of the plane rose to his feet, whipped off his hat and came down the aisle collecting money. Lisa smiled and I grinned like an ape and clapped him on the shoulder and he left. That was the other thing about his 'funnies'—they always took a sidewise swipe at the church.

As soon as he was gone I felt Liza's touch on my arm and realized I had been staring at the door through which Hobo Wellen had left. The touch told me it had been a long frozen moment; and what had been going through my mind during it, I just do not know. A growing, mounting pressure of some kind, yes, but a pressure of what? Desire, love, wonder, and was that anger? Why anger? And fear with many faces, not the least of them the certainty that nothing would ever be the same again, that I stood on the borders of a new country with a long journey to make. This part of the fear was not so much the sure knowledge that there was danger ahead, though I knew there was, for I knew that there was discovery and excitement and enrichment too; it was the fear of change, which is a very special thing and perhaps not fear at all, for life is change, isn't it? And why fear life?

"Dan!"

At last I looked at her; I took her elbows and looked down into her face, her dear face. Liza is one of those women who is the envy and despair of all the other women her age; she always had, always would look younger than she was and younger than all of them. It wasn't only the small, slender, firm body and the smooth skin and clear eyes; it was the way she carried herself, the way, when she moved or spoke, she released energy rather than stoking it up and eking it out like the rest of us. She kept her masses of blue-fired black hair rolled and folded up into a gleaming dark helmet and her eyes were not green, as they seemed to be, but an illuminated blue full of so many flecks of gold that they seemed to be green.

"Dan—what is it?"

What moves a man to do the things he does? Sometimes he knows before he does them, sometimes he knows at the time; but what of the times when he acts not knowing why, not understanding even afterward? She was frightened, and instead of trying to comfort her, or trying to understand or explain, I watched my own two hands living a life of their own, rising to snatch the big pins out of the sides and back of her hair so that it tumbled down about her shoulders and back.

"Dan!"

Why didn't I comfort her, why didn't I look for one single word to still the birth of terror in that face? Did I like it? Dan Currier, who, when he bumbled into hurting someone even a little, was almost obsessed with efforts at instant consolation? Or was it the certainty that whatever was going to happen would make up a thousand times over for any distress on the way?

She was trying to say something: "Dan, I don't know what you're thinking. If you think I was, if you think he— let me go. Let me go!" or some such. I kissed her, I corked up her words and her breath with my mouth. Her eyes, so huge and close, were big enough for me and a dozen like me to tumble into and drown; I tumbled, I drowned. When I released her she was crying; I'd seen her cry many times before but never like this, except maybe that once on the roller-coaster and the other time when I was in the accident and the radio said I had been killed and they were mistaken and I walked in the door without a scratch. I said, "Come."

She went with me willingly, bewildered, until she found herself at the foot of the stairs, and then she held back—not much at all, but even that little made something explode inside me. I picked her up like a doll and sprang up the stairs two at a time and crossed the upstairs hall as if my feet, somehow, weren't touching the floor; but we were at the top of an arc, having been thrown by some huge force. The bed was a blaze of gold from the tops of the two wide windows and a floodlight of sun; there was nothing on it but the bottom sheet, and I dropped her, or threw her down. She bounced, she screamed; I took her wrist and hauled her up sitting and broke the two top buttons off the soft denim jacket, then got hold of the hem and snapped it off over her head. She wore nothing under it, which was a vast surprise to me; I hadn't known, one way or the other —how could I? I punched her shoulder with the heel of my hand and down she went on her back; I snapped her waistband as if it had been a single thread and snatched her skirt off. Her sandals had disappeared somewhere along the way, and she lay naked in that glory of light. I had seen her naked before, of course, but I had never let myself look at her, really look, and as I got out of my clothes—it seemed to take forever, but it couldn't have been long, for I tore my shirt and ripped the zipper in my trousers halfway down; one of my socks, I found later, was still in its shoe!—I held her pinned down to the bed in the circle of my vision with her eyes tied to mine in the center of it. I was breathing deeply but not rapidly at all—strange, that—while her breath came and went like a pulse, making and losing shadows between her ribs and the superb taut hollows at the sides of her belly. And as I held her so, where she lay with her arms crossed over her breasts and her hips half-turned,

one knee drawn up to conceal herself, something from me
—a demand which was not anger, but still was like a fury
—reached out invisible hands and pulled those arms down
and away from her breasts, dropped the small strong hands
curled to the sheet, rolled back the hips, straightened that
leg. The sunlight (you take pictures in your mind at certain
moments) slanted down through the hair on the mound
between her legs and tinted the skin under it, making the
clear cream-color radiate up—a wonder. It was all a wonder, even in the violence and speed of the act itself, frozen
forever in the mind, ready to be retrieved forever after,
spellbinding, breathtaking.

Then I was on her, and it was all new: never before in the
light, never before in haste, never before with the eyes and
without cover, never before this smooth opening-up for
me, this unimpeded charge and plunge, for always with
Liza and me there was this long patient nudge and press
and slow yielding; if I moved too fast it was dry and hurt
her. Her gateway was completely wet and wanton . . . wanting, which was a glory too, because nothing, nothing, nothing on earth could have prevented my deep and total lunge
into her at that moment. Then another new thing: she cried
out.

She cried out . . . what was usual with us? We loved each
other, Liza and I, and she never denied me. Who had told
me that I must deny us both as much as I could, and that
when it became a pressure we must do what must be done
quickly and in the dark, and, though we embraced and were
happy with it, never discuss it before or afterward? And
during it . . . not a sound. Once—I recall it particularly
because it was the first time—after we had been married a
month, Liza gasped and held her breath, and it was as if
both her small hands were magically inside her, grasping
my organ and squeezing it rhythmically. When it subsided

she let out the breath with a long hiss, while her heart thumped my chest like something frantic, imprisoned. As for me, I demanded of myself a control that would make me silent as I climaxed; if I caught myself breathing faster I would instead breathe deeper until it was over. That, usually, was three or four minutes—sometimes a lot longer if I was tired or worried—and it was at those times when again I might experience that extraordinary breath-held tightening grip inside her, like her little hands; even then she controlled that gasp. But now—she cried out.

She cried out, and here was Dan Currier, professional (obsessional) consoler: a cry was to be heeded, the affliction of pain was to be stopped and existing pain consoled. This is everything I was and everything I meant to be. But now, at my first great delving lunge, miraculously made swift and easy, she cried out, and I withdrew almost all the way and lunged again so deep and so hard that it bruised my pubic bone against hers, and again she cried out, louder. Of course there was pain, that shattering drive of flesh into flesh and bone against bone, and my great weight on her and my big arms locked around her so that the cry was forced out as shockingly as it was driven out by whatever was moving her. How, then, she could take in enough air to do what she did I can not explain, but she cried out again and again, each cry like a plucked string, sharply appearing and fading, four, five . . . seven of them, diminishing. And with each cry, that incredible gripping inside, but harder, stronger than I had ever known it, so much so that I could realize, now, that I had not *felt* those earlier ones, but merely sensed them.

She was silent at last, and drenched with sweat from head to foot. I took my weight off her, raising myself on my elbows and placing my hands on the sides of her face and locking my gaze with hers. In hers I saw only a great wonder

—no fear, no pain—and in this and in the strange slack slightly swollen new shape of her lips, such love as I have never known.

I began to move slowly, deeply inside her, and then, like a slow-motion reenactment of that first great drive, withdrew almost all the way and pressed inward again, right to the root. Each time I penetrated to that depth her eyes almost closed, but not quite—not enough to sever the cable of withness that had been woven between her eyes and mine. We had never done this in the light before; we had never seen each other experiencing it; I think that in a deeply important way we had never seen each other.

She put her arms around me as far as she could, pressing and stroking my back, and then her legs separated widely and I felt, for the very first time, her heels locking down against the backs of my thighs: oh, she was strong! I hadn't known how strong she was.

With a deep and quiet joy I recognized the beginnings of my own climax, and here again it was new, new. For usually it was a rush upward toward the final explosion, with perhaps a split-second pause of almost unbearable sensitivity before the ejaculation—and that was a short series of electric thumps and a complete fall from whatever heights to the ever-present here-and-now. Thinking of the way it used to be, a phrase occurs to me: "I never left home." But now . . .

Now I rode no rockets to a quick burst of color and a cinder-fall. They say that when a three-hundred-foot tidal wave struck somewhere in the Pacific, fishermen eleven miles out were unaware of its passage, so gently and massively were they raised and let down. This is the way I was carried up to a height I had never before known; it was that all-but-unbearable point of sensitivity that I had flicked past so many times before; but this time I rested there forever, while time stopped. It was from this altitude that my joy-bursts were launched—not the abrupt sequence of little gouts of relief, but long sibilant syllables arcing up and out into a universe I had never known existed. Four, five of them, another, and then an interminable rest on that summit, and then one more, and then the last.

I had always been silent before; now, I shouted, and while that long wordless cry issued from me, another voice sounded deep inside me, as clearly as if another Presence shared the room, shared me, with Liza, and it said *"I am the way and the life."*

Then the great wave let me down, let me down peacefully and easily into the presence of my wife and my world and a sunshowered here and now.

She whispered my name and said something I knew, but always good to hear . . . and why she said it at that moment I simply could not understand, and did not try: "No other man will ever touch me."

I lay where I was, looking at her. Some small something in me was yammering at me to try to pick up the pieces . . . explain . . . apologize . . . make some reparation for this terrible conduct. Whatever it was, I broke it off and threw it away. There was a rightness about what had happened that needed no explanation. I smiled, and still deep in her, moved a little, and only then made a most interesting discovery. I had just experienced a veritable earthquake of an orgasm, but I was still rigid and ready. Full of delighted disbelief, I began to move slowly, gently.

Liza's lips spoke my name again, though somehow she had no breath for it, and now at last she let her eyes close. Her head tilted back, and there was born such a smile as I have never seen before. She clasped me close and moved with me, a kind of slow and knowing dance. Then *"Dan!"* she cried, and climaxed, and at the first strong pulse of that inner grip of hers, I came with her. It began somewhere below the calves of my legs and flooded upward and spilled into her while my head spun and the room went dark. *"I am the way and the life."* The voice brought me back to her; it was my voice, not one from inside my being, underlining a shout.

"Oh," she said, "twice. Oh, twice."

I had never been happier in my life, and I said so.

"Dan," she asked, "what was it?"

"Godbody," I said, and kissed her. "But don't ask me what I mean. Not for a while."

Liza Currier

I FELT WONDERFUL THAT morning, and in those days it frightened me to feel that way, and I'd much rather not. I put on the soft denim jacket and skirt and my sandals—that's all. I'd do that sometimes; he never knew, nobody did, I think, but the soft thick cotton felt so good against me. It was one of the little things I used to do, had to do, that made me feel a little guilty and a little, well, courageous and a lot more alive.

It was a beautiful day, not quite summer yet, with every leaf on every tree new and unmarked and with that freshly dusted look; late spring always has been the most troublesome time of year for me. It makes me feel a little . . . angry, I think is the word. To be a woman and the minister's wife and live in a town is—oh, it's nice, I mean it's a good thing to be and to do, but you're never your own person. Your house belongs to the parish and your time belongs to the work, and things you say and how you look and where you go are surrounded with little rules and do's and mustn'ts and can'ts that just don't apply to other people. So it's a little disturbing to feel late-spring wonderful on a bright warm morning.

And Hobo Wellen came over, he said to speak to Dan. He knew perfectly well Dan wasn't home; everybody in town knows that when the car isn't in the drive, Dan's out, and anyway, the kind of thing Hobo talks to Dan about is never anything urgent. Really, I get so mad at Dan sometimes; oh, not mad. He's so *good.* I get mad at that, I think,

30

not him. It gives him blind spots. It's hard for him to see that people like Hobo Wellen are not only superficial, but sometimes destructive. I mean, Dan's under attack from people like that, and he doesn't seem to know it, and when you tell him he starts listing the person's good points and makes you feel uncharitable. You see, Dan really believes that there's good in every person, every single one; all you have to do is bring it out. He's made me believe it too, but I also believe that some people are like mines that have gold in them all right—real gold, too—but it's down so deep, and surrounded by so much worthless hard rock, and is, when you get to it, such a little bit, that it's just not worth what it costs to get to it. I don't argue this with Dan, because it's the one thing we could never agree on.

Hobo Wellen comes on as Dan's friend, that's what bothers me. He's bright, you know, he found out very early in the game what sort of man Dan is. I think he found it out sooner, even, than I did when I first met Dan. Dan was a construction worker then, with no idea in the world that he'd ever become a minister, and we were friends, that's all, and he came to me the day he got his . . . what he calls his "tap on the shoulder." A lot of things fell together in his mind all at once and he just knew what he was going to do, and you don't stop Dan once his mind is made up. He went right back to school and fought it through; it wasn't easy, and then after he was ordained we were married.

It was during this time that I came to know this special thing about Dan: he is an absolutely convinced and sincere man, but his convictions are up for grabs. I mean he is so open, so, well, *reachable,* that if you can show him another way, convince him he's wrong, he'll accept your way completely and discard whatever he's been living by—discard it completely no matter what it costs him or anyone else. Which isn't to say that he's weak or vacillating—far from it.

All I mean is he's wide open and willing to test what he believes against all comers, because that's what keeps him sure he's doing the right thing. If you come along with something better, he'll accept it—but it had better be better.

Hobo Wellen picked this up fast, and maybe it was some kind of challenge to him, I don't know. He was willing to waste hours of Dan's time forcing Dan to defend some of the more awful things the Church has done—hanging witches, the Inquisition, things like that that don't matter any more—and things in the Bible that contradict one another. And dear sweet Dan would take each one as it came and deal with it seriously, never realizing that people like Hobo aren't serious about what they're saying, only what they're doing, which is to take down what other people have built. Maybe it was all because Dan was so big—Hobo is not a tall man. He has nice hair and good teeth and he always looks well dressed no matter what he's wearing, but next to Dan he looks like a bobcat next to a bear.

Anyway he came in that morning—when you're a minister's wife, everybody can come in—and I was washing the windows in the living room. He flopped down in the big chair and watched me; he had a way of watching rather than looking at you. He made me feel naked . . . it was more than that; he and late spring and clean warm air and sunlight all got together to make me feel, down deep inside, that I wished I was naked. He talked that way, too . . . it's hard to explain, but he could be saying one thing to you with words and all the while sending something else with his eyes; and that something else is not the kind of thing a married woman wants to be listening to. Not this married woman, anyway. I'd got it all straight with myself and with Dan and with being a minister's wife, and it hadn't been all that easy to do, and I didn't want it attacked.

So Hobo Wellen lay back in the big chair and watched me, talking easily, which wasn't bad, and sometimes falling silent, which was a whole lot worse. I was using a squeegee on a stick, and he made no effort to help . . . well, I wouldn't have wanted him to. But then while I was reaching up to do the top pane, I flicked a glance back over my shoulder and saw how he was watching the backs of my legs. Before I knew it I had knocked against the curtain rod with the squeegee and down came the whole array of fully lined double drapes. I must have caught at them as they fell, because one of the little L-hooks got bent, but I didn't see that at first.

Hobo jumped up and crossed to me. "Can I help?" He pointed up to the L-hook—not the bent one—and said, "All we have to do is hook it back up there." A stupid, obvious thing to say, but Hobo Wellen is neither stupid nor obvious. It was the old diversion-of-attention thing that every parlor magician knows. He pointed and I looked, and with his other hand he touched the small of my back.

It made me furious, because in one split second I knew what he was doing and what he had been doing. He'd been lying in that chair watching me work and wondering if I was wearing a bra—with me it isn't easy to tell because I don't sag and I'm not all that big. And he used this cheap trick to put his hand on my back and see if he could feel the strap. All right, now he knew, and I was wildly angry on a lot of counts: that he should find it out, that he should have done it so smoothly and without warning, that he *knew* . . . and I had to wonder what he thought of it and of me, and what he might say to me or to someone else, and what might come of that, and it made me angry to have to worry about those things too—not the things themselves, you see, but having to worry about them. And it all had to do with the choices you make, and not being able to live more than one life at a time except in your head, and being a minister's wife and the do's and don'ts and mustn'ts and . . . I snapped at him, "No, I don't need your help," and I hopped up on the table and picked up the rod with the heavy drapes. I got them on the one hook, and that was when I found out the other was bent.

I hung the rod and it dropped, and I caught it and hung it again and it dropped, and my arms were getting too tired and Hobo was standing very close by the table, looking up at me and knowing I wasn't wearing anything under my jacket. Then all of a sudden he shouted and grabbed me around the hips—it really wasn't until afterward that I realized that he grabbed me before I started to fall, that he made me fall. There was no way for me to go but right into him; I hung there half-balanced with his arms around my hips and his face thrust into my lower belly. He exhaled deeply, and I could feel his hot breath warming my most private self; my head spun . . . it was all flashes of Dan and how controlled he was, mixing loving up with decisions about good and evil . . . the spring sunlight, the do's and don'ts and the Tuesday Club tea for the Building Fund.

I don't know how long it lasted, poised, held there full of lightnings, ready to fall . . . and then he lifted me down and I pushed away from him, hard, feeling his hands still on me though they were gone, feeling his breath on my body though it was gone too; and there was the scrunch and chatter of Dan's wheels in the drive.

Hobo Wellen stood back and gave me a perfectly knowing smile. "That was a close one, wasn't it?" he said.

"Not really," I said sharply, but it was, it was; and then there was Dan, dear great cloud of clumsiness, bumping the side of the door with one big shoulder as he came in, the way he almost always did. I blurted something to him about the drapes and Hobo helping me; oh, damn it, I felt

I *had* to explain things, I felt guilty, but I hadn't *done* anything.

Had I?

Then there was some of Hobo's silliness, a story about an airplane crash, and as usual it was an attack, and as usual Dan didn't seem to see that. It was while Hobo was telling it that I realized there was something different about Dan. He seemed to be listening, but he wasn't; he was caught up in something . . . I kept looking at him: Good? Bad? Oh God, was he angry?

Then Hobo finished and left, and Dan stood there looking after him with the strangest intent expression on his face. "Dan!" But he didn't hear me. He really didn't hear me at all. Why was he looking at that empty space where Hobo Wellen had just been? Why didn't he look at me?

I went to him and touched his arm. He stood still for a moment as if he had something to finish first, and then he turned and looked at me. Oh, did he look at me!

What was he seeing? Drilling down into me like that, his eyes surely could see it all: Hobo Wellen, the touch and feel of him, the pressures of spring, the wild-wanting nameless things I had always felt but which had always to be suppressed, and the guilt they generated, guilt for things I had not done and would not, would not do . . . would I? . . . all the things he couldn't have known about but certainly could see now. And the expression on his face—was it anger? Could Dan Currier, of all people, be a jealous husband like those idiots in the movies, and jealous because of anything I had done or . . . or *was?* I began to be frightened. "Dan—what is it?"

He did not, would not answer; instead he brought up his hands and pulled the pins from my hair so that it tumbled down. I was frightened; he wouldn't *say* anything, and he had never done anything like this before—never. It was

Wellen, then. Dan thought . . . Dan thought . . . I started to say something: "Dan, I don't know what you're thinking. If you think it was, if you think he . . . " He was holding me so hard, so steadily; his hands were like manacles. It wasn't fright any more, it was terror.

"Let me go, let me *go!*" but he stopped my words, my mouth, my breath, my heart with a kiss. How can you live for years with a man without knowing he can kiss like that? And not for a second did he let me go with his eyes, so big and close they filled the world, they filled *me.* He released me, all but one hand, and said, "Come." I was crying, I couldn't see; he began to lead me. Then I realized I was at the foot of the stairs, and I held back.

What happened then is hard to recall, hard even to be-lieve. It was as if Dan picked me up from the corner of the living room where the stairs are and in one motion threw me on the bed in the second-floor bedroom—one great long breathtaking swoop. And it was a blaze of light there, with the high sun pouring in through the unshaded upper panes of all the side windows; the unmade bed, with only the fitted bottom sheet on it, was like a great snowy stage. Dan snatched my clothes away and for a moment I cowered, trying to cover myself; but though he stood away from me, busying himself with his own clothes, he held me pinned with those newly-lit eyes, and they seemed to command me to open, to show myself. I lowered my arms, my sheltering leg, and let Dan and the sunlight have me. Naked he came to me like a thunderbolt, uncheckable, unerring, and there was no time to fear hurt and hardly time for the great wonder that there *was* no hurt, none at all: I was as moist and ready as ever I had been in my life, and more. He surged into me with what must have been a crash, though there was nothing for me to hear or, indeed, to see . . . not then, not then. Nothing like this had ever happened before, not to anyone—I was sure of that—and sight and sound were sunken away in a great flood of touchness as he withdrew and plunged once again; and I met that, that single, second thrust, with a climax such as I had never dreamed of. Dan held still, deep within me, to take all I could give until it had passed, and then began slowly to move. Our eyes were still locked, and down inside his I could sense and share where he was going, up and higher, higher and up again, held in some transcendant place for—forever, perhaps?

Have you ever looked deeply and closely into well-known, well-loved eyes and seen them, unblinking, go blind? Not the blindness of dark, this, but the onset of unseeing glory; I knew he was with me as never before, but through me into an other-place, where he poised, waiting. And at last what he waited for came to him—not the effortful hammering of release that I had known before in him, but a series of long, measured spurts of ecstatic force, over and over and over, impossible but real. Even when they were over, he stayed in that high place interminably; I could sense reality and my presence as a person, not as a faceless force-among-forces, filter back only slowly. And at last he was back with me.

There was a strange thing, too: it was only with his return that I heard the echoes, and I actually had to trace them back into recent memory to realize that he had shouted. There were no words to this great sound he made, but words, or a concept, or an insight must have come to him at the same time; I know. I know Dan.

We were still for a time, soaked with more than the sweat and other wetnesses of loving; we were bathed in wonder. Then he raised himself slightly and took my face between his hands, and realized, I think, at the same astonished moment as I did that he wasn't finished, even after such an incredible release. He moved slowly, almost completely withdrawing, then as slowly coming in and down; we smiled at one another—pride, delight, compliment, joy, love—and together we turned ourselves toward this new experience. I let my eyes close because of the joy of opening them to see him watching me; I bent my legs around his to draw him nearer; I think, if I could, I would have drawn him completely inside myself, as if I could open my skin and close it again around him and be a single thing with him. It was in this feeling of mutuality that I began to realize that what was now happening was happening to us both, not to me and then to him, but to us both as one, and miraculously, I climaxed again—which I had never, never done before— and he did too, saying in a huge voice:

"I am the way and the life."

As the great wave receded I looked up at him and spoke my miracle: "Twice. Oh, twice. I have never been happier in all my life. Dan . . . What's happened?"

"Godbody," he said. I suppose I must have looked puzzled, because he laughed suddenly and kissed me. "Don't ask me what I mean. Not for a while."

So we lay there for a while longer in that little lake of molten sun, naked and unashamed for the first time together, knowing we had a world of it, new worlds of it ahead. We inspected and touched each other in the light, belated explorers and adventurers. We showered together, laughing.

Oh . . .

Hobart Wellen

I CALL IT THE Trick, and it works. Even if you don't score, you can see it working, and wherever you don't score, if you keep using it, you will. The Trick is something anyone can do, but most people don't know that. The Trick is, no matter what you're saying to a chick, you keep your eyes dead center on hers and you say silently, *You and I are going to make it.* You don't stop, you don't let up, and sooner or later they have to fall. You can see them wiggle and waver and try to fight back, but they can't, because most of the time they don't even know you're trying. They think it's coming from inside them, and when they think that, you've got 'em.

That Liza Currier now; oh, those tight little tits, how about that little muscular ass? That is quality stuff. She doesn't know what she's got, and that goes double for her big dumb husband. Him! He doesn't know it when he's being insulted, he doesn't know when he's being attacked, he's even willing to leave that little bowl of sugar with the cover off and a sign out. That big old blue Oldsmobile is either in the driveway or out of it, and when it's out, so is he, and it's like somebody banging on a gong and yelling, "Come and get it." Oh man would I like to pull him down, him and his "Can I help you brother" and the vestry board and the Tuesday Tea.

Anyway, there I sat with the driveway empty, watching Liza Currier wash windows with a squeegee on a stick, talking about the weather and doing the Trick. The way the

39

soft blue material of that jacket she was wearing went taut
and loose across her back was driving me right up the wall.
She had a beautiful way of moving. Everything was always
balanced, kind of certain. She smiled a lot. A mouth like
that, teeth like that, ought to be doing better things than
smiling over the weather. Then there was that tight little
ass, and the tapered legs ending in little gold-trimmed
barefoot sandals. I was appreciating those specially—sometimes I think the Trick works on skin as well as on the eyes,
and if you look up and down a leg just so, you might as well
have your hand on it—when she looked over her shoulder
and caught me at it, which was all right with me. Next thing
you know she'd jabbed the squeegee upward against the
rod and down came the drapes. I was over there in a flash
to find out what just had to be so: I pointed upward to
direct her attention away and put my hand between her
shoulder blades—sure enough, no strap. That did wonderful things to my crotch and filled me full of wonderful
things I would do to hers. Oh, but that would fix that big
stupid galoot Dan Currier; I wondered what he would do
about "finding the good" in me then, and saving both our
souls.

Liza was so sharp with me when I did the Boy Scout bit,
offering to help, that I knew she knew I knew; also, I was
wondering about the pants. She scrambled up on the table
and tried to hang the drapes back up. Fat chance: one of
the hooks was bent. That little squirming striving ass at
eye-level was more than I could stand, and I thought,
Hobo, now's the time for her to fall so you can save her;
so I yelled *"hup!"* like a circus acrobat and spun her and got
my two hands on the cheeks of the tight little tokus and
pulled her crotch right up against my face. I've found out
there are some things you can do, if they're crude enough,
nobody you do them to will believe you're really doing it.
There was a kid in Dan Currier's choir who would build up

to a sneeze and then holler *"horseshit!"* as loud as he could in the middle of the Te Deum, and nobody ever noticed. Another thing I found out is that if you can get the heat of your breath into a woman's crotch, you have her lassoed. So I let out a long breath into the soft denim against my face while my hands were discovering she wasn't wearing pants, either. The next thing to happen was for me to slide my hands up under the skirt, but just as I tipped her forward onto my shoulder there came the scrunch of gravel under wheels . . . oh, boy, the scoutmaster himself, coming home on cue. I lifted her down as if I was a gentleman and set her on her pretty little legs, and she pushed away from me. "That was pretty close," I told her, and she said, cool as you like, "Not really." But it was.

Then in he comes. He had a vaguer-than-usual look about him and ordinarily I would cut out at a time like that, but this wasn't ordinary; I was enjoying Liza's upset too much to leave just yet. So I told him the airplane joke, though I don't think either one of them heard me, and bid my adieux and left. The last I saw of her that day was the way she was looking at him, as if she had something to confess and didn't know what, and didn't know how. It was funny.

Part of it wasn't funny. I don't like to get handed off by anybody or anything when I'm that close to a score. I tried the old philosophy bandage: once you get a frau pulsing up like that, you can come back in twelve years and go on from where you left off, or just about. But that didn't help much now. I began to feel something I hadn't had since I was a teenager—a lover's nut. Like having a C-clamp slowly closed on your balls and then walking away with the clamp still hanging there. Every step I took I felt it more, and Dan Currier began rapidly to become my most unfavorite character.

I thought over the prospects. Mostly I hate going back

over old ground—it's the road ahead that turns me on. But this early in the day most everyone's at work or school, unless . . . . By then I was just passing the *Mountain Star* office, and a voice jumped out at me and blew all my plans away, leaving me with only the lover's nut. "You, Hobo. Hobo Wellen!"

I went in. It was just a storefront near the end of the main drag; half of it was a gift shop. The *Star* is one of those weekly local papers full of lost dogs and old houses for sale, cheap at twice the price, and big local news: Tommy Zweck had an eleventh birthday party, Jim Breeze's parents from the city spent the weekend. And, of course, the gossip, Mrs. Mayhew's gossip, *The Little Bird told Me . . .* Mrs. Mayhew was the little bird, and she wrote bird-talk: "Fluttering down Jason Lane last night I saw you-know-who with a new one, dressed in blue and, really, far too young, don't you think, Mr. You-know-who? And what do *you* think, *Mrs.* You-know-who?!" Always that "?!" Or: "Somebody's big white Buick convertible was parked ever so late outside a certain someone's house the other night. Didn't know I was perched in the old oak tree, did you?! But I won't tell. (There's a pine tree on the same lawn, though.)" She knew everything that happened everywhere in town, Mrs. Mayhew did, and she used to brag about how she didn't tell all of it. And she didn't. Some things she just threatened to tell, which is how she got so much information. There was hardly a person in town who didn't have that goddam little bird flying over his head ready to crap on him if he didn't behave himself. Why do you think I right-turned real smart and marched in there?

And sure enough, there she was, and Mr. Merriweather from the bank, sitting out his lunch hour. Merriweather and Mayhew, the M&M's, the kids used to call them, guardians of morals and decency. Talk was that the bank never lent a penny without checking with Mrs. Mayhew, who checked with her Little Bird, and people could be made or broken by her and her rumor-box and never know why. . . . Did you ever hear that people who live together a long time get to look like each other? Well the M&M's had grown to look like each other over the years, which was funny because Mr. Merriweather had a little bowlegged wife called Isabel who, if she looked like anything, looked more and more like the toy poodle she lived with; and Mrs. Mayhew was a widow of long standing and lived alone, her and her Little Bird, which of course was caged up in her head. All anybody remembered about the extinct Mr. Mayhew was that he had more money than God.

Anyway, you can add something to that folklore about people looking alike after living together. People who live alike get to looking alike too, even if they live apart. Mr. Merriweather and Mrs. Mayhew were both pushing fifty, and both had the same pouches under their eyes, the same slightly yellow eyeballs, and the same lines around the mouth that you see on aunts and spinsters who never fuck, but instead suck on nothing all the time while their juices dry up. They both had slightly greying hair, and each had a single fore-and-aft wattle from chin to Adam's apple. Both of them had eyes that protruded slightly but were down in caves: deepset pop-eyes, that says it. They had exactly the same voice, but one octave apart. They approved the hell out of each other and disapproved of everything and anything else. Oh, God, the damage she did with that column.

I remember one time some kids were sitting on the porch steps across the street and the girl, about fifteen, bent over and kissed the boy, but I mean on the cheek. Mrs. Mayhew had been sitting in the back of her office for half an hour with the light out watching them because they were sitting close together, and the next issue of her column had a crack by the Little Bird about "open and public displays of affection on the village street. How about it, Sue?" and little Sue Vines, known now for "what she was" by the whole village and everyone in school, ceased and desisted, and the next time she snuggled somebody it was under the bridge down at the creek and she got knocked up.

As for me, she'd never published anything about me, but she knew something, and even though the girl got better and no longer lives around here, Mrs. Mayhew knew and I knew she knew, so when she said "Come," I came. It was a real drag sometimes; either she had an item and wanted me to confirm it, which I couldn't always do, or she needed an item and if I didn't have one, I'd have to make one up. Maybe some of those made-up ones did damage too, but you know something? Whatever you say about people is probably true, and if it hurts them, mostly they deserve it.

"Well, Hobo," she says on her trumpet, "how nice of you to drop in." She enjoyed this kind of thing. "Any grapes on the grapevine?" I just shrugged and shook my head. She looked down at the portable typewriter on the desk in front of her and so did I; it had one short paragraph on it and then a wide space. I got the message. She needed material. God damn.

I said, "Well . . . " and looked over at Mr. Merriweather. He was leaning forward a little and extruding his eyes. His lips were open a bit away from his two big rabbit teeth. Mrs. Mayhew had two big rabbit teeth in front too. She wouldn't let me con her off; she said, "You can speak freely in front of Mr. Merriweather, Hobo dear. My, if you can't trust your banker, who can you trust?"

There's an answer to that, but I wasn't about to give it. I looked at the door and heard the typewriter carriage move to start a new paragraph. I got that message, too. She meant to get something out of me and she was perfectly willing to pin my poor aching balls to the wall until I gave it to her.

"Well," I said, and then I had this inspiration. "I can't say for sure, I don't know anything, it's just a feeling I got, but I think there's some kind of trouble at the Curriers'."

"Oh," she said, "Oh, how awful," and she smiled; she kind of hunched over her typewriter with her talons out like a vulture wondering whether a carcass is dead enough yet. "What kind of trouble?"

"Oh, gosh, I wouldn't want to say." I came on like a real gentleman with ethics and all. That taken care of, I went on, "I think it's something to do with some guy who hangs around the missus while the pastor's out pastoring."

The smile became a grin. I looked at the banker; he had a grin too. I stopped thinking about vultures and began thinking about hyenas. "Go on, go on."

I got very sincere. "I really don't know any more, who it is or anything. You can't make an item out of that, Mrs. Mayhew; I don't really know anything."

"You could find out," she said, her head still down over the typewriter but her eyes up and aimed at me. Ever see one of those anti-aircraft guns with two muzzles side by side, poking up out of camouflage? That's what it was like, looking down into two ringsights showing through eyebrows. So I said, scared, but was I laughing inside, "Well, I could drop in a little more than I do, I guess."

"I suppose you could," she said, which meant "Do it!" and I could have laughed out loud; the one worry I had about hanging around Currier's was that she'd get wind of it, and now I was so safe from that that she'd skewer me if I didn't. "Which doesn't help me a bit with this week's column. What else, Hobo?"

I racked my brains. I ought to be able to say something

about somebody in this town. I had to get out of there; I was carrying a cargo of baled barbed-wire, and I had to dump it, quick. Part of my head was still running down possibles, the Shetland girl, Dona, old Betty, Bugsy Schneider, that goofy Wanda with the sewed-up lip. There was something wrong with them all—too young, too old, too dirty, too noisy, or I'd just been there before and who needs it? Joanna, Margy, Britt . . . *Britt!* Hey, why not two birds with one stone? Really, why not?

I said, "Well, it really isn't anybody's business, is it? I mean, how could it hurt anyone even if it's so? It's not as if she lived on the main stem or anything."

"How could what hurt anyone? Who?"

"I'd rather not say," I said real firm.

"Admirable, Hobo. You're absolutely right not to tell. What is it that this Miss or Mrs. X does?"

"Well, I heard she sunbathes in the altogether."

"You mean without even—"

I nodded. Mrs. Mayhew looked at Mr. Merriweather, and he looked back at her, and you know what? All four lips were just as wet. "This early in the year?"

I'd heard it last year, actually, but I tried saying nothing and it worked. "Right out where the children might see," Mrs. Mayhew said to her typewriter hands.

I answered that: "Yep. Any kid wants to scramble up a quarter mile of creek bed and then climb half a mountain so's they can look down," which gave her the exact location.

"Oh," she said, *"her."* She rubbed the talons together. "Well, she'll get her warning, in no uncertain terms, the baggage." That's the word she used, baggage.

I said I had to go. Mrs. Mayhew frowned at the blank part of the paper in the typewriter, and my hopes fell and, from the way it felt, landed on the load dragging on my scrotum.

Then Merriweather spoke up. "You could warn them both—her and Mrs. uh, I mean, the minister's wife."

She considered it, and then looked at me. "All right, then, Hobo. But keep your eyes open." That message said, Boy, you better have a respectable load next time, or else.

"Sure will, Mrs. Mayhew, you bet. 'Bye." I waved at them both and got out of there.

I walked home and got my wheels and drove up to the quarry. After that it was creek bed on foot, and I began to wonder if this had been such a great idea after all. A lover's nut is something you can sleep off, or you can hammer your meat and get rid of it, but if you have something lined up and you're getting close, it gets worse and worse and that is no time to be climbing over rocks.

Britt was some kind of a Skywegian, a female hermit, kind of, that used to paint pictures and stick old burlap and twigs and things on them; somebody said she was pretty good and once or twice a year would sell one for a bundle. If she ever had a bundle she didn't use it on making herself comfortable. She had a little house built smack against the rock wall of an abandoned hillside quarry. There was a kind of shelf of land in front of it with a spring that made a pool like what a farmer will dig for a duckpond. The roof of the house was built way out, like a porch with no floor, and held up with a lot of uprights that she had trained vines all over, so it was hard to know if you were in or outside. Up on the hillside, if you wanted to risk your neck and the chance of making a lot of racket in a shale-slide, you could get where you could look in her windows and a kind of skylight thing in the roof. That was how the rumor got around the year before about her being naked: some kids were up here.

I don't mind winding up with a final sprint when I'm after some nooky, but I've learned the hard way that you better be sure of the ground—all of it—before you make your play. If I could look in and size her up first, I would. I could, so I did. By now I had a lot of mileage and trouble over this, and it had to come out right. But at these prices it had better be good. So, all right—I had ways of making it good.

I got to a place, all scratched and bruised and out of breath, where I could hang on to a tree root and stand with only one foot on a rock, and lean over just one inch this side of the topple-point, and I could see into the one big window at the side and also down into the skylight. And I have never been so surprised in all my entire life.

Part of it was because the story those kids giggled out last year was true. I never expect good juicy stories to be true —hell, they don't have to be, if they're juicy, who cares? But sure enough, that kooky Britt did go around bare-ass. Or at least, that's how she was when I looked down.

The other part of the surprise was Britt herself. I guess I'd seen her in town a hundred times, maybe carrying a picture in a gunnysack, or trudging back up into the hills with the sack full of groceries. We have more than one oddball in our town, artists and writers and musicians, and it's all right as long as they keep their place, attract the tourists and don't get rich. (When an oddball starts making real money it makes other people try to be the same kind of oddball and that upsets things.) Anyway Britt used to go barefoot most of the time and dress in a kind of tent and wear a thing like a junior-league tablecloth over her whole head. She had great big blue eyes with heavy lashes and eyebrows, and she couldn't hide those; otherwise what could you say? Regular teeth, straight nose, a lot of chin. But oh, look at this:

Hair dull gold, down almost to her ass. Big firm tits without a sign of sag. The longest legs I think I've ever seen on a woman, and almost no body hair at all. I couldn't believe my eyes. Then, the skin. I guess she did sunbathe naked after all, because her whole body was a reddish-gold color without strap marks or pale places. That, friend, was a whole lot of woman. She was moving around the place, cooking something, I think, and every now and then tossing back that big plume of hair. I don't know how long I hung there on the rockface watching her . . . watching her . . . I do believe I forgot for a while what I had come all this way for. Can you imagine? What reminded me was a sharp pain in the back of my leg and a shift in that one foot; I was *this* close to just using it up and having it quit and sending me down into her yard in a heap of shale.

I had to edge back to a wider shelf and cling tight to the rock wall for a bit, to get my breath back and my leg too. There was a civil war going on in my balls, heavy artillery and bayonets as well. Now, that just had to be taken care of.

I backed down to level ground and banged some of the dust and dirt out of my clothes and hair. Okay, now for the sprint, because the coast was not going to get any clearer.

I got into that thicket of vines and uprights under the overhang of the roof and worked my way around the side of the building. There was a small window to pass, and through it I could see her standing, reaching up to light a candle swung from a chain—not that it was dark, but the house was in the shadow side of the mountain, and the skylight opened to the main part of the house. It wasn't but a second's glimpse, but the tight muscles of her belly and those lifted-up breasts and the fine, scarce down between her legs revealing the pink slit and the rounded lips made two explosions inside me, one in my head and one in that battleground downstairs. I all but yelped from the pain, and scrambled around the corner to where the door was. I meant to have me a slice of this, and I meant to have it *now.*

What I was going to do, see, was kick the door in and just dive. Then she'd freeze, or she'd run; either way I'd get to her. No woman can stop me when I get like this. They hand it over because they're scared, or they try to fight back, and that's even better because then they get the old rabbit punch and I cold-cock 'em and just leave it in 'em and wait for them to wake up. Only . . .

Only this time there was no door to kick open—it was open already. And I didn't get to dive in—she came out. I guess she was stepping outside for something on the porch just as I came around the corner; anyway, there she was. Finally, she didn't freeze and she didn't run. She just said, "Hobo Wellen! What do you want?" (only she talks kind of funny, and it was more like " 'Obo Vellen! Vot do yew vant?") and took a step toward me.

I made no speeches; I downed my zipper and took out my tool. I was breathing hard; that's the way I get. She looked down at my cock and up again at me, and damn it, she didn't seem sore, she didn't seem scared, she just was kind of . . . puzzled. Well I could fix that. I grabbed her left wrist with my right hand and pulled her hard toward me, and with the edge of my left hand I cut her hard on the side of the neck, and down she went. As pretty a sight as I ever saw, the way she sprawled down on her side and then twitched over on her back, putting both hands where I'd hit her. I could've carried her inside where it was more comfortable, but I like it better this way, here on the packed-earth floor. Maybe later I'd take her in, but now, from the second I chopped her, my dong pulsed up hard; it took only four heartbeats for that to happen, and you can bet they were fast ones. It came up like it was hooked to a hydraulic pump, or like four frames of a movie film, from limp to rock hard.

The woman was moving a little, vaguely. I kicked her legs apart and fell on her and found myself looking at a foot.

It was a great big foot; looking back, I'd say a size eleven or better, and there was another one like it close by, and some ankles, and long-boned, big-muscled calves and knees the size of my two fists. I rolled off Britt and goggled upward, and there was a man standing there, a naked man, a redheaded, big-jointed man with a slab-sided face and funny-colored eyes and oh God why is it always a big guy in my way?

I jumped up and tried to say something, but I was half out of my gourd, and all that came out was a funny squeal. I jumped back out of the way, and it was like somebody hit my poor swollen nuts with a bat; I had to hold them. The wonderful big hard-on just disappeared the way it does with a scare, and I jumped back again, absolutely out of range of those long arms and big hands. I wanted to call the son-of-a-bitch a son-of-a-bitch, but all I could manage was another one of those squeals. I scrambled backward holding my balls, tripped over something and almost fell down, backed away some more, and then turned and ran away down to the creek bed.

I guess I ran farther than I had to; he wasn't chasing me, but I didn't know that. When I more or less came to my senses I was more than a mile away from where I'd parked —I'd turned the wrong way—and deep in the woods. I dragged myself up out of the creek bed and got out of sight on some moss behind some bushes and kind of put myself together. I had a cut on my leg I didn't remember getting and scratches on my arms and a place on my hip that was going to be one great big sunset of a bruise and I couldn't remember that, either. Most of all, where I hurt was in the crotch. My poor balls were throbbing like a couple of misplaced abcessed teeth. I looked at them and was only amazed; maybe they were a little redder than usual, but that was all; but the way they felt they should have been swollen big as basketballs and crawling and jumping around inside the skin.

I did the only thing I could do: grabbed that little limp

dick and started to jerk it. It hurt—everything hurt. My hand hurt the cock, and the movement hurt the balls. It wouldn't get up, either. It just stayed limp as a dirty sock. But I couldn't stop; I had to drop that load, or I'd never make it back into town.

I don't know how long I lay there with my back against a tree, pounding my meat. I closed my eyes and called for all the help I could get from what I could remember and what I could imagine. It was all a big mix inside my head, and whatever helped—Britt reaching up to light a candle, that chick I nailed down by the bridge and banged half in the water, Liza Currier's smell when I shoved my face into her crotch, and more—those things would no sooner stir up a little hope and begin to stiffen my cock, when they'd remind me of tires on gravel or size-eleven feet or the sound of a police siren or something else, and I'd lose it again.

But I couldn't stop, and finally I made it. I have no idea how long it took; I only know that when I was done the skin was rubbed off on one side of my goddamn overcooked-macaroni superlimp prick, and sweat-salt was rubbed into it, making it sting like hell, and when I came it wasn't in any way a pleasure. You can come out of a limp dick; it isn't easy, and it doesn't spurt but drools out like the spit out of a cow with hoof-and-mouth disease, and the way the balls tighten just before it happens is, if you have what I had then, one big gruesome agony.

I fell asleep, right there in the woods, and slept for the rest of the day. I was in a hell of a shape when I woke up, but at least I could walk without going bowlegged.

Britt Svenglund

YES IT HAS BEEN lonely these years, but why is it when people say the word "lonely" it has always to be like a bad thing, or sad? You go alone after you have been hurt, to get well, like a forest animal. Then is getting well a bad thing, or sad? No. Mr. Currier said in church, one of the times I went there, any person who cannot be by himself, it's because when he is by himself he thinks he is not in good company. Also I read a little book once about the top of the soil, just the first six inches under the grass, and everything that happens in it. If you have a ten-power microscope and if you take the time and care, you could spend all day every day for more than a year seeing and understanding all the things that are happening in just one square foot of topsoil. There are plants and animals and chemicals growing and changing all the time in a tiny world like that. There is a fungus which makes a noose with a trigger, and when small creatures come into it, *bang!*, the noose closes and catches them and the fungus eats the animals. There are eggs that hatch and insects that make certain scents to call other insects to love or to die, and much more, so much more— all in one square foot of dirt. So how can anyone with eyes to see and a heart to question say he is bored, there is nothing to do?

Summer and winter I work and read. In the summer I warm my body under the sun, and in the winter I watch the fire and think. Whatever I need, I make it or do without. Some things I must buy—flour and salt and soap and

53

books. Paint. For my work, almost everything I need can be found. That is because of my art secret.

My art secret is this: there is only one sense, and it is the sense of touch. All the other ones are just kinds of touch, the same way the scientists say that matter and energy are only different kinds of the same thing. Most of the artists in the world who are, or whoever were, were painters. That's good, but a painter's work is meant not to be touched. Sometimes you should not, sometimes you must not, touch the work. But I have my art secret, and so when I make a picture of a mountain I make the sky of a piece of silk, and the mountainside of bark and bits of stone and sand, and water of glass or bits of plastic I sometimes find. Oh, yes, I make colors. But I could make a picture of a mountain and a sky all the same color exactly, but because the sky was silk and the faraway hills were burlap and the near ones bark and stone, you could see the picture anyway. Also sometimes I mix honey in my sky color, bitter roots in my sharp rocks, smooth spices like allspice and paprika in my smooth stone, mint and sage in my greens. You can put your hands on my work, you can put your mouth on my work, you can smell it here and there. So, then, why is it bad or sad to be alone? I am not sad when in the morning I look up into the sky and taste it and when I know the feel and smell of the faraway hills. Also I have my goats and a wild apple tree, and things grow for me in the garden, little green promises that, in good time, are kept: *I will give you tomatos, I promise you corn.* People do not always keep their promises even when you tend their soil. Sometimes they do, but you never know. Also when a bee stings or a rock falls and hurts you or a knife cuts you for being careless, these are not really attacks. These things are defending themselves or they are giving you the results of causes— there is always a reason. People sometimes attack you without a reason, and you never really know when, so it is better not to be with people. Some boys climbed the hill behind my house and saw me naked, and they threw stones. That is not a reason, you see.

The sense of touch is a crystal with many faces. Air explodes away between the hammer and the anvil and disturbs the air around it, which in turn disturbs the air again, and these disturbances walk toward you like footsteps until they touch the membrane of the ear. So it is too with the rush of sound through the stiff feathers of a crow and the soft ones of an owl's wing, and each has a different meaning. To see is to touch also, and to be seen is to be touched, and this too has its many meanings. To be seen by a cruel boy with a stone in his hand is not the same touch as being seen by a stag or by a squirrel. If you live as I do and know how to touch and be touched by eyes, you can feel eyes upon you even when you cannot see them, and you can know what kind of touch it is.

I knew there were eyes on me when I went to the garden to gather a handful of chives and a few leaves of tender new lettuce, and all I could tell about the touch was what it was not. It was not the touch of a deer, which—to me on my mountain—is not fearful but merely alert; nor the touch of a rabbit, in which you can feel total terror and, in an instant, total forgetfulness; nor the squirrel's contact, which always has laughter in it. What touched me was not the gaze of a carnivore either: wildcat and fox browse you with their eyes like shoppers, wondering and judging whether or not they can afford you. And if this touch was that of a man, it was such a man as I had never known.

It was such a man as I had never known.

Once in my first winter in this country I saw a bird for the very first time, on a cold morning in which there was only white which was altogether white, and black which was altogether black. And this bird was all the color in the whole universe of that place and time—this bird was a clear and aching red. I have come to know it well, since, but this was my first one; they call it cardinal. My feeling then was more than joy, it was pride, for I thought at the moment I had produced the cardinal, invented it. It was in my mind as I saw it that I had made it be, by a necessity born of a world of total white and absolute black . . . oh, please, laugh at this arrogance of mine, laugh with me, as I laughed at the time, and laugh now to think of it, that I felt I had the power to create a cardinal.

Now, in a world of many greens and browns, under a sky that must taste like the inside of the skin of a concord grape, and the passing shadow of a macaroon cloud, the man appeared. He stood just off the path between the garden and my house, and as our eyes met he stepped back a pace —a message that he would not bar me—and he smiled, which was a message that I need not fear him, for he feared neither me nor himself. He was naked, but he . . . oh, what are the words? . . . he wore nakedness like a garment; he wore it better, I think, than I. Light lay on him like a fabric, and air, tailored to him. He was umber, amber, ocher and gold. The modeling of his face had been done with a flat tool, and beautifully finished, for it was all planes and rounded joinings, and brows, eyes, and lips all parallel. His hair was red of a kind, his eyes another red, his skin a series of others.

And the difference between my seeing this man and my encounter with the cardinal was this: there was in that first blazing glimpse of him no slightest feeling that I could have created him, or anything like him. I am artist enough to acknowledge the necessity of a cardinal in the snow. I was not, I am not, capable of such a concept as this man.

I tossed back my hair in fear that even a strand of it might interfere, and stood with my hands full of tender young green and, nested in them like songbirds' eggs, the very first radishes. We stood quietly looking at one another and then he crossed one ankle before the other and sank smoothly down to sit cross-legged on the grass. He placed one hand, then the other, on his knees the way I might put down brushes I did not intend to use just now. I walked by him neither quickly nor slowly and went into the house. I put the greens down on the kitchen table and put my forehead against the rough boards of the wall and closed my eyes. I could see him again that way, vividly and in all his colors, so I did that for a time.

Then I went back and stood just inside the doorway and looked out at him. He had moved. His long arms were around his shins and his head was down, his forehead resting on his knees. He was absolutely motionless; he is the only human being I have ever known who could be that. I went softly down the path to him and stood looking down. His hair was quite a different color from the cardinal's feathers, but still and truly a red. His upper arms were heavier, I thought, than they should be for a man so tall and lean, and the forearms were corded. I have seen such forearms on dairy farmers and on smiths, when I was a little girl. It became unbearable, after a time, not to be able to see his face.

I sank down on my knees near him and spoke to him; I asked him who he was. He raised his head and looked into my eyes for so long I began to be afraid they would dry, but I would not close them or look away.

He said, "Godbody."

I told him my name. He nodded as if he had known it all along and was pleased that I had told him the truth. Then he said, "Was talkin' to a man this morning who told me his name, and it didn't mean anything at all, not the way he said it. I had to put my hands on him before I knew who he was."

He meant something he did not say. He did not have to say it. He meant that when I spoke my name he believed me, he understood who I was. There are no words to say how very much this pleased me. I think that almost every word we speak to anyone is a way of trying to explain to them who we are, and almost always we fail, and that is why I would rather not try. It is a great wonder to be able to speak a single word, your name, and be believed. There is only one of you in all the world, there has never been another, there never will be another, and once you know this, it is a hurtful thing to be taken as someone else or like someone else. You begin to try very hard to announce yourself to everyone knowing in your heart that it is as foolish as proving the existence of the sun, or water, or pain, and as useless as trying to disprove any of them. It is because I will not knowingly be either useless or foolish that I speak to no one unless I must. Yet here was a man who believed that I was I when I spoke my name to him, and it made me grateful to him and to want to do something for him, if, if only, oh if only he would accept it.

I asked him, "Will you eat with me, Godbody?"

He nodded and smiled. Why is it people, even artists, think that a smile turns up the corners of a mouth? It does not. The lips become longer. When he smiled his brows and his eyes and his mouth were still parallel. I went into the house.

I make heavy bread, the kind they call "black" though it is not, and I like to bake it before the sky lightens, these early summer days, because the baking warms the house when the sun-to-come stirs the air and chills it, yet the stove is cold when the day grows warm. This morning's bread was therefore still warm and soft at the heart; I kissed it for its forgiveness before I broke it, and put the pieces on my earthenware plates with some goat's cheese and the young lettuce shredded up with the chives. I made the radishes into little roses and dressed the salad with soured wine and a little of my precious olive oil, stirred in a rough wooden bowl with a clove from the garlic I keep festooned from the beams and a pinch of sea-salt. I put out the stone jug of goat's milk with its wet cooling-cloth. I had only the one mug, but we could share that. And there were russets taken from the hole in the ground where they had spent the winter; ugly little things, but mellow and sweet inside.

When it was ready I went to the door to look at him for a time, and to call him. He had moved again. He was standing by the path looking out across the valley and up. There was a cloud there sliding along the skyline, and I think it pleased him.

"Godbody."

He continued to watch for a time. It was like waiting for someone who is speaking to finish a sentence, or a reader to complete a paragraph. He had a politeness to that cloud which demanded the same thing from me, and I was willing to grant that in exchange for the gift of watching him. The high sun threw the great muscles of his wide chest into fine relief, and highlighted the three strong cables over his lower ribs, and put his strange eyes under heavy eaves, and filled the crisp hair of his loins with sparks. Then at last he and the cloud were done with one another, and he came smiling up the path to me. I was moved to hold out my arms, and he came into them, and we kissed without haste or passion. What we performed was a rightness, that was all, and then hand in hand we came inside to the table. While we ate he did not kiss me, yet that greeting kiss remained firm and sweet on my mouth during the entire meal, and everything that passed my lips was seasoned with it; there never has been such a flavoring for a feast.

My bed is a mound of spruce tips, and on these is a

rectangle of canvas, and on the canvas a smaller rectangle of wood, and held inside this frame are five wonderful old goosedown quilts from the old country, and the time of year will tell you whether to lie naked on them or to get under one, or two, or three, and the smell of the spruce, and the sound, tells you when it needs replacing, which you can do winter or summer. At the end of the meal I rose and took his hand, and he came with me to the bed.

We had not spoken since I called him. Asking and answering, pleasing and thanking, presenting and explaining —why? We had all we needed within reach: food, each other, the bed. Most especially we had no need for the second great use for speech, and the one it is most used for —to fill in the empty spaces between communication. There were no empty spaces.

We lay quietly in each other's arms for a long time, not exploring, not stimulating. We were waiting for something. Several times I have been to a Quaker meeting, and this waiting was very like the silence that descends on such a meeting when God is invited and whomever He touches may speak. I do not know if Godbody or I first became aware of the sunbeam, or just when each of us became aware that the other was sharing it. It does not matter; somehow we entered together a place of total attention on something else besides ourselves, which made us far closer than we could have been otherwise. To fix one's attention on another is to separate "I" from "thou." To share is to use another's eye and mind and senses.

In the window on the uphill side of my house is a box of earth, and on that day three tulips grew there, two yellow and one scarlet, looking like lollipops. The sunbeam passed over one of the yellow ones, touching its tips, and probed into the heart of the red. As it moved, the light drove through the petals, at first barely escaping the layers and emerging as a rich dim deep claret, and then moving upward and intensifying through cardinal to a blazing orange. Somewhere during this amazing passage I looked away and into Godbody's eyes, just once, and it was not away at all, for in each of them, in their cinnamon deeps, was repeated the burning chalice of the tulip.

And when the sunbeam had passed, he had entered me. It was done by no sudden thrust, no ritualistic preparation, no forced-draft excitement. His manhood simply grew into the womanness of me, erected into me. Our lower bodies were locked together, and a mere turn of my shoulders under his hands brought our eyes into each other as well. We lay on our sides, enfolding one another, interpenetrating, absolutely connected.

Then I wanted to move. Then suddenly, wildly, I desired to move, but before I could, before the desire could be manifested at all, his huge hands slid down my body and closed on my buttocks. He held me to him so hard I all but screamed; he held me, tied me, imprisoned me, and with his eyes he held me even harder. I understood then that this thing would end as it had begun, by its own growth and strength and not by any persuasions by either of us.

And grow it did, the pressure and depth of his presence inside me, the grip of his huge hands, the tempo of the hearts which pounded at one another through their cages of bone and flesh, and the temperature of those incredible eyes of his. Then I, oh then I did scream, I screamed aloud, short and piercing, and again and there was no pain in it, and I screamed and through a haze of red I saw his red eyes turn upward, turn and half-close and come back to me again and "Ah-h-h!" he cried, and we burst together in flying fragments of cinnamon and ocher and cardinal and carmine, fire and flame, flight, and finally fall.

Oh there was a dip then into a place where there was no

feeling because feeling is only the means of attaching that place to the outside. Oh.

Then the hands, though unmoving, were only gentle on my body, and our eyes were strangely full of tears. Perhaps that was because we were here again instead of that other place. But there was joy in being here again, the house, the tulips, the earthenware and the sudden bleat of a goat outside, for in that nameless place was a Presence so awesome that one could not stay, so great that one could be only insignificant, only a nothing which could never again merge into selfhood again. Oh, I know what I mean, but I do not have the words.

He moved his head back from mine, still holding me close, and he read my face, chin, brow, each eye, my mouth. He smiled and closed those incredible eyes and instantly, I think, fell asleep still smiling. I lay watching him and the way the light lay as a glaze on his moist cheekbone and jaw, and as fireflies on his lashes, and curled threads mingling with his hair. Inside he was dwindling, withdrawing not by moving but by becoming smaller, and though the sensation was exquisite it filled me with regret, and I tried to hold tighter; and that seemed to move him away and out of me even sooner. So I let go, let him go, watching him sleep and recalling to myself that of all our possessions there is only one which cannot be taken away from us, and that is memory; to let a beautiful moment slip into memory is only to keep it, not to lose it. Let the moment pass . . . let go . . . let go; it is yours for always.

I slipped away from him after a time and went into the kitchen corner to hull some berries for him when he should wake. Perhaps I should have felt eyes on me then—perhaps I did, I don't remember. I was too full of what had happened to be aware of anything else. I remember stopping to think, what would be perfect when he wakes? What special flower or arrangement of vines would be right to meet his eyes when they opened? And I thought, flame—only that. Flame, so I lit the big candle. Then perhaps something would be blooming now that I had missed seeing in the morning, so I ran outside, to come face to face with Hobo Wellen.

I had known him—seen him; I don't believe we had ever spoken. Some of the women and girls in town watched him like children looking at a wolf in the zoo, giggling and frightened; the sillies, they did not know there were no bars. I never thought him so noble a thing as a wolf, he seemed to me only a sick man. He had about him a neatness that nothing could change, not even now, breathing so hard he grunted, covered with dust and earth. I called him by name and asked him what he wanted, and his answer was to open his clothes and take out his penis. I do not believe that anything God made on any living thing is disgusting; but this was, not for itself, but for the way he handled it and glared at it and at me. It was a very large one, I think, and limp.

Then he took my wrist and pulled me toward him, oh . . . It was so unexpected. He hit me on the neck and I had a great shower of stars on a grey background, and the mountainside wavered and swung up on end, and I was lying on the ground, and Wellen flung himself on me. I had no time even to be frightened. The blow was shock, not pain. Then there was pain, but something else: Wellen had ceased to move. He lay on me with his face close, staring away at something I could not see. I looked too, and it was Godbody, standing over us, his face quiet. Perhaps his eyes were longer, narrower than before. He did not speak.

Wellen scrambled to his feet and I sat up. Wellen made a long swine sound, a *oeeeeoink!* and ran away backward. He fell and scrambled and scuttled like a spider and got up again, holding between his legs and again *oeeeoink!,* and he turned around and was gone.

I turned my head to look at Godbody, and under my hands, which were still one on the other on the place Wellen had hit me, there was a terrible stab of pain. He knelt beside me and gently took my hands away and ran his fingertips over the place. At the base of my neck and on the shoulder a great knot was forming. He put his big hand on it, snuggled it so that the contact was firm, and with his eyes took hold of mine in that way he had.

Something began to flow, I could feel it like fluid, leaving me and entering him. It was pain turned liquid and running out of me into his hand. I could tell by his eyes and a tightening of his face that he felt it as pain, too; he was taking the pain out of me and bringing it on himself. When I realized that, I made as if to pull away—oh, why should he, *he,* take my pain? But pulling away from Godbody is like pulling away from a part of yourself. He knew what passed with me, and he would have none of it; the hand on my neck and shoulder was welded to me until he was finished doing what he was doing.

For he had healing hands.

At last his hand came away from my shoulder and neck and he sat back on his heels, tiredly, his shoulders slumped. It is a burden to have healing hands. I took the one which had healed me, and he winced and then smiled as I lifted as gently as I could and covered it with soft kisses. Ah well, loving is not healing, but perhaps it is the next best thing. Yet he would carry my pain in his hand until it went away in its own time.

He helped me up, and we went back inside. I let him sit and watch me while I finished with the berries, and then we took them with the cool jug of milk and the stone mug and shared them.

The sun was gone from the tulips, but the way they looked, they remembered it. I lay down and Godbody lay next to me, close, with his healing hand on my breast. I said part of the sun was still in the tulips; did he think the sun would miss it?

"Oh no," he said. "It's been used. The flowers make it stronger. You got to be used, your arms, your legs. You strap a man's arm behind his back," he told me seriously, "it will turn into sticks and skin in a couple years." He looked at his hands, and then he stroked me with them. "You got to be used, all over, everything. You get stronger."

I thought of Wellen. I do not know how Godbody knew I was thinking of Wellen, but he said, "He just don't know how. He can't make it with a woman unless he hurts her. Didn't you see that?"

I didn't know what he meant.

Godbody said, "He got a hard-on when he hit you. Not until he hit you. And he hurt too."

I looked deep down into those strange, warm eyes and saw the pain there. I understood suddenly that in the presence of pain, Godbody shared it, took it and kept it. I asked him a puzzling thing; I asked him, "Did you take pain away from him?"

"I could of." He thought about it for a time behind his eyelids. When Godbody closed his eyes his lashes lay right down on his cheeks. I watched this and waited.

He opened his eyes again and said again, "I could of, but he ran away."

"But you would?" I think, for the first time, I surprised him by one of my questions.

"Well, sure!"

I thought, the man is my lover, and Wellen hurt me. Then why would he help him? And again Godbody seemed to hear my thinking because he said, "He was hurting. He hurt in his balls and his guts, and he hurt in his head."

And I thought, is that an answer? And immediately: yes, it is. What do you do if someone is screaming and screaming and will not stop? You try to stop it, any way you can. (Unless you are another kind of person and hold your ears and escape.) Pain to Godbody—anyone's pain—was like a scream, and he needed to stop it, most especially because he was one who knew the ways.

But then . . . why did Godbody let him run away with his pain?

Godbody put his arms around me. "They got to come to me," he said, "like you did."

Did I? Did I? Oh, yes I did, as he sat by the path to my garden, hiding his face. Was his face, I wondered, the way it was just now when I saw it sharing Wellen's agony, and when I saw the injury to my shoulder flowing into his hand?

Had I been screaming, screaming, in some way? I with my life so separate and well-ordered in the company of my green things and my sky and the animals of the hillside? I shouted—it was a demand—I shouted and shook him: "Godbody!"

And as usual he understood me perfectly: "You was lonesome," he said.

Willa Mayhew

Flitting along the highways and byways of our dear little village I am surrounded by bursting bud and spreading leaf and the ~~clouds orchestras~~ choruses of birdsong, and you don't need to be a bright-eyed little bird to know that spring is fully here. ~~Perching dancing bobbing~~ Stopping on a twig to rest and look around a little the thought comes to me that everything grows a little in the springtime, good things and, oh yes wicked ones too.

Oh, yes, wicked ones too. I sat back into the familiar squeak of my desk chair and looked out into the springtime. It was pushing in through the window at me, swelling and pushing. There in the little window beside me was a tight green bud of boxwood, bent over and tapping against the screen, and it looked just like the head of a you-know-what, pressing and pressing to get it. They look very tender and sensitive, but they're not, they can push in anywhere; you can't stop them, they're so persistent.

I bent over the typewriter and looked at what I had written. *Flitting along the highways and byways.* Our dear little village is a cesspool, gentle reader, and every time anyone draws those dimity curtains it's on devil's work—thought, word, or deed. They've got to be watched, they've got to be stopped. For their own good. *I* don't care. But some people know the difference between mankind and the lower animals. Andrew Merriweather does, at least I think he does, well, most times I think he does. Well, I am tolerant. You have to be tolerant toward anyone who carries one of those you-know-whats stuck on his body. It's a sort of parasite. It has a kind of life of its own. It moves by itself. Edith told me about the seventh-grade boys, how that happens to them sometimes, and she knows they don't want it. She always makes them come up and write on the blackboard when she sees it. She says they get embarrassed and scared, and she believes in "association." She says if they get embarrassed and scared every time that happens it will associate. Then it won't happen, even when they're alone. I know what they do when they're alone. They all do it. Oh, if I had a son I'd never let him be alone, not for a minute, even if he had to sleep with me. I would see to it that he thought about other things.

> Wickedness can send out shoots and bud and flower, just like good, yes, and bear fruit. This little bird knows how bitter the fruit is, not from personal experience, ha ha!!

Ha ha. If I had any personal experience I would not be so perfectly qualified to do what I do, for thank God I am without taint.

My dear departed husband with all his money was a dirty old man, and he made up his mind to do it to me when I was only fourteen years old, and for two years he kept his eye on me, and when I was sixteen he made Mama say I could marry him. Mama never told me anything about what men did and bless her for that, I certainly know why. That one night I thought that old man had gone crazy, trying to touch me all over and showing me that big pushy you-know-what. I tried to get away, but he was strong—much stronger than anyone knew—and he held me down and put the, you know . . . oh, I don't know what made me think of all that again. I won't think of it . . . I fainted and when I woke up he was lying on top of me and I called his name and said, "Get off." At first I thought he had fainted too. He was so heavy, and I was still, you know, like that with him, but it was not the same.

I got up and took a turn around the office, and decided not to think about that again, and that made me feel better. I sat down again at the typewriter. The hard bud of box-wood went press-press-squeeze against the screen. Then it was still. I slid the screen up and felt it with my thumb and finger. It was cool . . . . The old man lay on top of me for a long, long time and then I touched his neck. It was cool. It was cold. He was cool-cold inside me.

I suppose I screamed. Somebody said, "Mrs. Mayhew, are you all right?" I think for a second everything was whirling around in my head, then and now, a thirty-five-year-old nightmare, the office, the dead old man on top of me and in me too, the paper in the typewriter *personal experience ha ha!* and it all cleared up and I was standing there with the broken stem of boxwood in my hand and there was a little cut on the side of one finger and there was blood on the bud. I mashed it and shredded it and threw it down and I felt as if I had run a long way. I turned around and looked at Melissa Franck, who was standing there flut-tering her plump little hands together and looking out frightened from her thick glasses and saying, "Mrs. May-hew are you all right?"

"Of course I am, can't you see?" I suppose I spoke sharply to her, because she winced. I looked down at my hands, red blood, green blood, shaking. There was shred-ded spring-green all over my typewriter and the desk. "Do that to all of them, there would be a lot less trouble in this town," I said, I don't know why, and went to the sink in the

back to get a band-aid and wash my hands. The whole time
I was at it she must have been trying to puzzle it out because
she suddenly called out, "Oh, was it a cutworm?"

"Yes, it was some sort of a cutworm."

I came back to the desk. She had tidied it up. I sat down
and looked at her. I wondered as I had wondered before
how a skin as smooth and unmarked as hers could look so
unhealthy. She was one of those strong-featured, square-
jawed people who are timid and squeaky-voiced. She always wore loose sloppy sweaters and knit skirts that kept
right on sitting down after she stood up so nobody could
tell what shape she was. She dressed as if she were ashamed
of it, and well she should be. She'd been raped. She knew
who it was and I knew who it was too, and she knew it.
Nobody else knew except, of course, *him.* I don't think
there was a day in her life she wasn't afraid I would tell or
put it in the paper. I could get a lot of work out of Melissa
Franck. . . . It was funny how I found out; it just shows that
it pays to have the bird's-eye view, ha ha. Only one glimpse
of Hobo Wellen talking to her across the street and the way
she laughed. Then the next day she came in cool as you
like, but sort of holding herself together. Extra busy, you
know what I mean, and always looking down. So I made her
come right to my desk, I made her look right in my eyes and
she couldn't, not for more than a second or two. So I said,
"So that's it!" and that's all I needed to do, she started to
cry, and after that I had her and she will do anything I want
her to do for fear I'll say or write something about her
getting raped and everybody will think she's bad. Melissa
Franck bad, imagine that! . . . Then, of course, I let Wellen
know I knew. All it took was a glance at Melissa's back one
time when he was in the office, and he knew all right.

I keep a pretty tight watch on Hobo Wellen. I just have
to know who is good and who is evil in this time, and Hobo

Wellen is a walking proving-ground. Just watch people, especially girls. In the Old Testament it says many times that woman is the vessel of evil, and this is what it really means: that girls are silly. All girls are silly, but some pass a certain point in silliness and that is where the evil begins. You can tell—well, *I* can tell—just by hearing one of them laugh, sometimes merely by the way they walk, when a young woman is right at that point of silliness. Now if you had a piece of chain to test or a sample of dyed material or a shovel or a new kind of bread, you would test it to destruction—pull it till it breaks, boil it till it fades, tear, pound, pull apart, bathe in acid. Hobo Wellen is the acid test, all I ever had to do was point him at one of the silly things and it wouldn't be long before I knew. I could name more than a dozen women and girls, right off, that I have tested that way in the last two years, yes, and eight of them did not pass.

Seven. I've got to be fair. No one ever could say I was not fair. I won't know if it's eight until I hear about that Britt, but I know what I'll hear, the hussy, exposing herself that way. Oh well, to work.

But we don't have to eat the fruit of evil. We are people, not animals, aren't we? (Well, *I'm* not, but that's different!!) And one of the differences between men and animals is that we can learn. Haven't we learned yet what happens when we eat the evil fruit? Of course we have!! We have learned too that the fruit doesn't have to ripen, and if I may coin a phrase, we can nip it in the bud.

Flitting about here and there, day and night, I can see where the buds are. Oh, they grow where you expect them to grow—from seeds left by the city trash that comes up here to teach our fine young people to take dangerous and deadly drugs and to defy all the laws of God and man with their horrible hair and their beads and filthy talk. All that comes from Communist countries. I know because I have had many a serious talk with birds-of-passage as they fly through our dear little village, and they tell me so.

But the seeds of evil have been planted in places where you least expect them, too. "Eternal vigilance is the price of liberty," and it's the price of law and order and it's the only way to nip the fruit in the bud once it is planted. Suppose I told you that a flower of evil was blossoming this spring right in one of our houses of God?! Why else would someone who should be blameless (and who shall be nameless) be receiving such EXTRA SPECIAL attention from a certain person when her husband is out earnestly doing the Lord's work?! Why is a certain citizen, accepted for years in spite of her—well, eccentricities!! (isn't that a beakful of a word for a little bird like me?!) —why is she permitted to parade indecently on one of our hillsides where our young folk might at any time be defiled by the sight?

You see, this is what is meant by "eternal vigilance." It isn't only a matter of watching the invader. Anyone can do that (though not many really do, do they?!). You have to watch the things you've been sure of all along and the people you have always thought you could trust, people that should not, could not (?!) do wrong. Washing clean is good—but you have to wash clean every day, don't you?!

So keep yourself clean in every way, and when other people—and little birds!!—watch you, just let them and feel glad. And you watch other people too, and if ever you see the tiniest little seed sprouting where no seed

should be, you know what to do, don't you?! Just whisper
it to your little bird, and you'll get a thank-you. And
nobody will tell on you, ever ever. Until next week—
tweet-tweet!

I leaned back into that familiar squeak of the chair and
took the typewritten sheets and put them together and read
them, and I was pleased. I thought, that will show her, the
little slut. The Rev. Currier is a man I never could quite
understand. Now Mr. Grudgeon, who had the church before—he was a man one could deal with. I think it was
because he could get angry, and because everything was
very simple for him—good and bad, God and country. Daniel Currier is always willing to listen, and I really don't think
that's a good thing in a pastor. A leader should lead, not
follow; talk, not listen. A preacher should preach. A sermon
is not what Daniel Currier calls a "dialogue." I was suspicious of him from the first. Well, from the first time I saw
that slut. I never had a chance to get at her before, so sweet,
smiling all the time. The thing is, the thing really is: no
minister of God has the right to marry a cute-faced little
slut. There are four churches in this town, and she's the
only preacher's wife who looks like that. She has no *right* to
look like that, and that's where it really is. And he had no
right to marry her and bring her here. If some man has
started hanging around her it's just what was to be expected. And I don't care if Wellen is lying, because sooner
or later it had to happen, and we might just as well dispose
of Mrs. Goody-Goody Liza Currier before it gets to be a
real scandal. Then maybe we can get someone in that pulpit
who preaches like a preacher, married to someone who
looks like a preacher's wife.

I think I laughed just then—I do when I feel good about
something—and I looked up into Melissa Franck's silly

face. She was pulling at her own fingers harder than ever, and the end of her nose was very red, which is what always happens when she's upset. Behind her big glasses her eyes were going blink-blink-blink very fast.

I said, "Are you finished typing it already?"

And she began to stutter, which is the other thing that happens when she's upset. "N-no, and I'm nah-nah-nah-not g-going to either."

"You're *what?*"

"I d-don't care."

"You know that copy's due at the print shop in thirty-five minutes."

"I d-don't care."

"You know if it's not ready they'll go to press without my column."

"I d-don't care."

I looked at her. I have found that with some people all you have to do is look at them, keep right on looking without saying a word—especially if in an argument it's your turn to talk—they will have to say something else, and it's usually something you can use to defeat them. Well, it made her talk, sure enough. She held up my copy and waggled the pages.

"You c-can't do this, Mrs. Mayhew."

I said very carefully and distinctly, "Melissa Franck, are you telling me what I may or may not do?"

"You can't do this a-a-about Mrs. Currier." The end of her nose was even redder, and mercy, I think it was wet too. I pointed a long, slow finger at the pages she held in her hand. They were trembling: my, I could hear them from where I sat! I said, "There is not one word in that copy in any way referring to anyone by name. If you put constructions on anything there, it is your horrible little mind, not mine."

Then she surprised me. She shouted! At *me!* "That's what you think, that's what you always say anyway, but you know better and so does everybody in town!" And my, she forgot to stutter! She said, "There are four churches in this town, or three and a temple. Father Conklyn's a priest and hasn't got a wife and neither has Rabbi Brummel since Mrs. Brummel died, and nobody's going to think you are writing about Mrs. Fleckenstein, so who else could it be?"

I stood up. I am much taller than Melissa Franck. I pointed at her desk and typewriter, and I said, "You are not here to question what I do. You are here to do as you are told. Type that column, and do it now."

When I stood up she jumped back perhaps half a foot, but she stood up a lot straighter. She did not answer me. She merely raised the tip of that silly wet, red nose a little bit.

I said, "You know what this means."

"I d-don't care."

"Give me the copy."

She tore the pages right in two, and put the pieces together and tore them in two again, and put them down on my desk.

Somebody screamed as loud as they could, "You fucking cocksucking little shit, I'll run you out of this goddam town!" and I really don't know who it was, but it made my throat hurt as if something was torn in there, and I could not see for a moment, and when I looked up I was alone in the office. I sat down at my typewriter and put paper in it. There was a tick-tick-tick at the screen and another smooth, cool, round bud was pushing and pushing at me.

Melissa Franck

I NEVER, EVER, EVER did anything like that in all my whole life before. Melissa stand up. Melissa sit down. Melissa pick up your things. Melissa go to the store. Yes Miss Standish. Yes Mrs. Steiner. Yes Miss Grandy. Yes yes yes Mr. Miss Mrs. Harris Boyer Petrilli sir ma'am. Yes Mother. Yes, right away, Mrs. Mayhew.

And I was never late and I never missed a day of school, except for the mumps, or failed a subject, but nobody ever said see how well she does it, nobody ever said be like Melissa Franck, I guess because I never won a prize, made the honor roll, got the highest mark, even once.

Also nobody ever laughed at me for poor-kid's clothes or dirty fingernails or socks or a funny nose, but nobody ever said oh, what lovely hair or see the way she walks. Nobody in all my life ever said get out of here, but nobody ever said I want you.

Except him, that time.

But it wasn't really me he wanted.

I hurried along Maple Street after Mrs. Mayhew screamed like that. She was going to tell it all now. But it was worse, she was going to tell it her way. She had a way of telling how a person bought a loaf of bread or brushed his teeth that made whoever it was sound like a devil or pervert. Then what would she do, what would they all do, when she told about what happened with Hobo? Even if all she told was the truth, everybody would spit on me and talk about me, and all the men would think they could have me, and I would have to say no, no, no until I got tired of it and began to say yes, yes, and then soon nobody would ever ask me any more, just laugh, because that's what happened to Sue Vines, and after she got pregnant there was the accident. Only I know it wasn't an accident, she opened the door of the car and stepped out into the road at fifty miles an hour, and it was only then that Tommy hit the tree. So you see you can get dead when Mrs. Mayhew takes out after you.

She went out after Sue Vines because she was so pretty, that's really the reason, so young and pretty. She pushed her down a little and when that made Sue go down a little more she pushed again and kept on until there wasn't any Sue Vines any more. So what would she do to me after what I'd done?

I looked behind me and hurried faster. Mrs. Mayhew was not going to wait to write something about me in the paper and wait for people to read it, and write more and wait more. Oh no, she would think of something much worse, much faster. I looked back again. I would not have been one bit surprised to see a whole mob of townspeople running after me with torches and Mrs. Mayhew egging them on and waving a coil of rope. But all there was was a big station wagon, coming along slowly.

I was right at the edge of town by then, at the crossroads where Highland Road comes across and Maple Street turns into County Summit and becomes a dirt road winding off into the mountains. I guess it was right there I decided not to turn right or left, which would just take me back into town. I just went straight ahead and left it all behind me.

So of course the station wagon speeded up and rumbled off the blacktop and pulled up alongside me.

I set my face ahead and tramped on.

"Melissa. Melissa Franck!"

Oh . . . Mr. Currier. Oh, I didn't want Mr. Currier now. I said, I suppose rudely, "What." Period not question mark: "What."

He didn't say anything, and I had to turn and look at him and then come over to the car. I didn't want him around me now because he is a nice man, the kind of nice man you can't just go on being rude to. If you did he would think it was his fault, not yours. So if he wanted to give me a lift I would say no, and if he wanted me to tell him what was wrong I would say no, and if he wanted to take me back there I would say no, and no, and no. I was really ready for him. "What."

"Do you know a man called Godbody?"

Oh.

I looked at Mr. Currier very carefully to see if this was a trick, but it wasn't. He really wanted to know, and he was not interested in me or why I was there or where I was going. I suddenly felt very normal and real again. I said, "I'm sorry. I don't, Mr. Currier."

"I'm sorry too, Melissa. I really am. Well—I'll just look around. 'Bye." He smiled.

" 'Bye." The car began to move and I began to cry. I don't think I have ever been so surprised in all my life. I know I was upset, but then that sudden thing of feeling normal, that feeling of being Melissa Franck, nobody ever cared even enough to say get out of here, oh there's Melissa Franck, we'll ask her where to find Mr. Godbody, if she knows, fine, if she doesn't, we'll go on looking, 'Bye, and forget Melissa Franck . . . this Melissa Franckishness that came on me, instead of calming me, it made me cry. I knew then that this was not a day like other days, and that whatever the change was that made me stand up to Mrs. Mayhew was a permanent change and . . . and . . . and things would go on changing with me.

Mr. Currier stopped the car and got out and walked back

to me where I stood crying. He held me. I think it was because I bawled Hoo Hooo Hoo . . . all the air going out of me and then something stuck and I couldn't get it back in and I was going to fall down. No man ever held me before, except—

I got some air, it scalded as it rushed in but it cleared things up a little. He kept an arm around me and took me to the car. He was a very strong man. I put my feet down one after the other, but I don't think it would have made the slightest bit of difference if I hadn't. He opened the right front door and put me inside. He left the door open and got around the car and into the driver's seat. I hunched there and blubbered, and all he did was to open the glove compartment and pull out a box of tissues and put them in my lap. I have no idea how long I huddled there like that with Mr. Currier resting his hands on the steering wheel and looking out through the windshield. I know it could have been much longer and he wouldn't have moved until I was quite ready. That man gave me those minutes. I mean for all those minutes he wasn't doing anything else. That never happened to me before either.

After a time I guess I was quieter, because he asked me if I wanted to go back to town. I shook my head because I was afraid I would start that awful Hoo-hoo-ing if I opened my mouth. He must have known this because he just gave me some more minutes.

Finally I said, "I'm not going back, I'm never going back, I can't." Then I said something that seemed to mean much more than all that; I said, "I won't."

He looked at me and then through the windshield again, ready to wait some more. I guess I began to feel guilty about that, and I said, "You have always been so nice to me, and Mrs. Currier is the kindest, prettiest, nicest lady in the whole world."

He smiled a little and said he thought so too, and "Is that

why you're leaving?" I think he meant it as a sweet little kind of joke, but I said yes.

He was looking at me again. Mr. Currier has a special way of looking sometimes, a I-don't-understand-that-at-all kind of look, lost and perplexed, like when they brought him to see the cats the Crendy kids had wired together by their back legs and hung over the clothesline until they killed each other. I said, "Mrs. Mayhew is going to say something about Mrs. Currier in her column and I wouldn't type it, and now she's after me."

He looked back down the empty road, it was a way of telling me nobody was after me. He just didn't understand. I said, "You don't get away from her if she's after you. Like Sue Vines. You have to do what she says." I looked up at his face, and if I could have laughed I would have. So lost.

I tried to explain it. "Mrs. Mayhew knows a lot of awful things, and if you do something she doesn't like she will put it in the paper and then everyone will hate you." That wasn't enough. I tried again. "I can't go back now—I've had a fight with her, she'll tell everybody."

"Tell everybody what, Melissa? I'm sure there's no 'awful thing' about you that anybody would believe."

"Yes there is," I said.

He didn't pry. "But then what is she saying about my wife?"

"That a man is around there all the time when you're out."

"Lots of people come in and out."

"That's not what she means and you know it." In spite of myself I was getting a little mad at him, I think. People shouldn't walk around so defenseless, thinking the world is good and people are good. It isn't. They just aren't.

"But there's nothing like that. It isn't *true!*"

"Mr. Currier," I said to him with all my heart, "Just the

way you say that—'It isn't *true!*'—sounds like true or not true makes a difference. Well it doesn't! It isn't whether or not a thing is so, it's what people say. People like Mrs. Mayhew anyway."

I always thought about Mr. Currier that nothing could shock him. I mean people really tried, you know, and it didn't work. He would just try to understand, or he would get puzzled. But I do believe this shocked him—what I said about true or not true, it makes no difference. I think he had been hanging on to that all his life—if you could know the truth about something, that was, well, *it.*

He said, "Melissa, something . . . " He swallowed, he couldn't get it out. He tried again. "Something is . . . happening." He looked at me through those glasses; his eyes were too big, looked at that way, blue and—and clean. Nothing not clean should ever be in a blue like that, eyes like that. "Will you help me?"

I was astonished. "Me!"

He said, "I know what it is, but I don't have the words for it yet." He laughed. "That sounds crazy, doesn't it? Here, let me put it this way: you know something I don't. Mrs. Mayhew knows it too, and Mr. Merriweather. Sometimes I think my wife does, but I'm not sure."

I let him think for a minute and didn't say anything. He was wrestling very hard with something inside him. He sort of threw up his hands a little and shook his head. "I can't."

I said to him gently, "Say it wrong."

"I beg your what?"

"Say it wrong, Mr. Currier. I mean if it comes out wrong you'll know it, and you can say it over different until it's right."

"I never thought of that." He looked at me as if I'd suddenly changed clothes or grown taller. "That's good," he said. "That's very good." He thought for a bit. "Well then, it's as if everybody I know, almost, knew a language I didn't know, or maybe words from some language I'd never learned. And they—you—all of you understand each other instantly, and I can see that you do, but I missed it. Well, then, I met a man this morning. Godbody. You don't know him. He—he touched me." He put his hand up under his open collar and touched his own shoulder. "And when that happened, the thing I always thought was true . . . *was* true."

I didn't understand him, but I didn't dare say anything. What he was trying to say was too important to him. So he went on, "It was true in a way I have never known before. And what that means is that up until that moment, all the things I have believed and preached and tried to make other people believe just aren't so. No, that's wrong. They are true, now. They weren't before." He looked at me very eagerly, searching to find if I understood. I just kept looking straight at him. He said, "When I was a construction worker I never dreamed I'd be a minister. Never in the world. And then I got the call. I really did. It was a very strong thing. I went back to school. Years. It was hard, too. But I didn't mind because I believed in what I was doing."

"And you don't any more."

"Oh, I do!" he cried, and then, "But I don't. I—I mean that I am a minister because I believe in God and I believe that God is love. And the Golden Rule. But now none of the rest of it seems to matter so much—maybe not at all. Not parishes or districts, maybe not the Bible, maybe even not the cross." He gave me a funny twisted little smile; he hurt. "There, I think I've said that right. That man touched me, and that's all I'm left with: God is love, and you must do unto others as you would have them do unto you."

"That's *all?*" I marveled. "That's a lot. It's more than I have."

He turned to look at me—straight out of his eyes at me and not inward the way he had been doing, and he was angry. That frightened me for a second until I saw that he was angry at himself, not me. "And here I'm getting help from you, when you're the one needs it!"

I said, "That's all right, Mr. Currier. Nobody can help me."

Then we turned together. Someone was coming out of the woods, along the creek bed.

It was that Britt Svenglund, who Mrs. Mayhew hated so much. She wore the down-to-the-ground dress she was always seen in, or one like it . . . but there was a difference, somehow. Maybe it was the material, or maybe it was the way she moved this afternoon. I don't think I had ever been aware of her body before, or of her having one. But then, I don't know that I'd seen her climb rocks before either. Anyway, as she gained the road and saw us and stopped, there was a difference I know I was sure of; she looked simply beautiful. I can't say why. She'd always had a nice face, nice straight nose, chiseled mouth, but . . . but this was something else. She—she *glowed.*

"Miss Svenglund—hello."

"Ah, Mr. Currier." I think she liked him, the way she smiled. He said in that marvelous open way of his, "You look wonderful today—wonderful," and she gave him none of this coy "Do I really?" or "What do you mean?" She smiled even more and said, "Yes."

He looked at her and at me, I thought apologetically, as if he had no right to think of anything but me just now. But he asked, "Do you know a man called Godbody?"

If her face was glowing before, now it seemed to release a burst of light. "How did you know?" What a strange answer. And when I looked at Mr. Currier, he was exchanging something with her with his eyes—it seemed like something very glad. Funny; he'd just been saying something about other people having a language he didn't understand. I felt very left out. Britt Svenglund said, "You too?"

Mr. Currier said, "I want to see him again. Do you know where I can find him?"

She nodded but said nothing. I asked, "Who is Godbody?" and I guess my left-out feeling showed in my voice, because they both turned to me as if I had stubbed a toe.

"You should meet him." Britt Svenglund said nothing, and they both looked at me, pressured to say something. Mr. Currier suddenly found what, I suppose, he would call his manners: "Oh, this is Melissa Franck. Do you know each other?" We did, a little. We nodded a little.

And then Mr. Currier said again what he had just said— said it like a brand new thing. "You should meet him." He turned to the woman with real excitement. "She should, you know. She really should. Miss Svenglund, Melissa is one of the good ones. Really she is. And—Melissa, do you mind?—she's in trouble right now and very unhappy. And it isn't her fault, it's other people. I think Godbody . . . " He sort of floundered to a stop. Again they both looked at me, knowing something I didn't. I thought, they're not going to make me do one single thing that . . . and then I kind of floundered to a stop too. It was the way they were looking at each other.

"I've got to go into town," she said suddenly. "He's at my house. He's sleeping." A beautiful small smile came and went. If you just listened to her words, they would be saying No, you can't see him. But if you listened to the way she said them, she was saying, Mr. Currier, I trust you and if you think it's right for Melissa to see Godbody, I'll help. And he answered in the same language, "I'll take you in, then." Britt Svenglund walked around the car and stood by my door. "You know where my house is?"

I shook my head. She said, "Go up the creek bed until you see some log steps set into the bank on your right. Just go on up."

"I can't," I said, "I just can't, I don't know him. He doesn't know me. He'll think . . . and anyway, he's sleeping, you said so." But while I was blurting all this I was getting out of the car. She got in and closed the door. "I won't be long, Melissa," she said and smiled, first at me, then at Mr. Currier. They were doing a thing that pleased them. Mr. Currier started the car and backed it around. I stood where I was until the sight of them was gone, and the sound of them was gone, and there was nothing but mountain shadow and the voices of the forest. I didn't know what to do. I certainly didn't want to do what they wanted me to do. I wanted to run away, the way I had been doing when I was interrupted. I said into the evening, "No. No!" and then I climbed down the bank and started up the creek bed.

Who is Godbody?

He became the crooked creek bed ahead, he became the loom of the darkening mountain shoulder, and around a turn of the bank he looked like shelves cut into the earth with split logs set into them, a winding stair. Up, and turn, and turn again, and the air became lighter, lighter out of the shadows, lighter to breathe. Godbody's up there: where? In the little house nestled against the hillside, with three times the roof a house needs, just to shelter some of the outdoors and bring it inside. Godbody's there. I hear the soft bleat of a kid and the cry of a mouse; an awakened owl ghosts between me and the house (as a gnat can fly between raindrops so can an owl fly between one sound and the next, carrying silence with him). Somehow all this is Godbody, only because if I say, where is Godbody? I must point to all this and say, there.

I moved under the wide eaves breathless, and it wasn't

the steep stairs alone that had winded me. Who is Godbody? An open door and a shadowed kitchen ell with a
great burning candle swung from a chain; and as I walked
under it on feet educated by the owl's wing, I stopped and
let the candlelight's soft dartings, the suffused late skyglow
through the windows and roof-light, say yes, say yes, there
is Godbody, there he is.

Who is Godbody? Long limbs, long body, long hands
relaxed and defenseless, unconcealed, abandoned to a
bodily, mind-ly completeness. Everything fit Godbody,
limbs to body, light to skin, his grace to his strength, and
the colors of skin and hair and eyes.

Eyes. Open.

I put my two hands tight together and stopped breathing.
I was very frightened.

He came up sitting with one easy motion. If anyone else
had done that (but then, who else?) I would have said he
was pretending sleep all along, but I knew that Godbody
had passed from total sleep to complete wakefulness in a
blink. It taught me too that doubtless he slept the same way,
instantly and altogether, when he was ready.

He spoke to me.

"Hi. Who're you?"

"Melissa."

He put out his hand. I went to him and knelt. I was not
afraid that he was naked, but I was filled with a new something. New to me. I think it is called awe. And I had never
seen a naked man before. He put his outstretched hand,
strong and warm, on the side of my neck by the shoulder.
"Yes, you are," he said. I knew what he meant. He meant
I had said I was Melissa, and he believed me. I cannot tell
you all I mean by this, but there it is.

"She said I could come to see you."

He understood me. He always understood me. "You
want to tell me about it."

I hadn't known that, but I nodded. He did too, and got up, taking my hand so I got up too. "I want to show you something first," he said.

"All right."

"You'll have to get out of your clothes."

I couldn't believe what I heard then. I couldn't believe it, my own voice, instant and easy, saying again, "All right." (Who *is* Godbody?) I took off the white blouse with the silly lace trim down the front. It was never silly before. I took off the belt and the pepper-and-salt straight skirt. (That's what those skirts are called, but they were never straight on me, not after the second time I wore them.) I took off the bra-slip and my pantyhose. He didn't look at me, he didn't not look at me. When I stood on one foot to take off the hose, he put his hand on my shoulder to steady me, and when I didn't need it he took it away. When I was finished I turned to him and he took my hand.

He led me through the kitchen and outdoors, along a little path to a garden at the edge of the bit of level ground on which stood Britt Svenglund's house. We stood together on a point of rocky ground looking out at a day dying and a night being born.

He squeezed my hand a little and smiled at me. "What's it like?"

I said the only thing I could think of, the single overwhelming thing I felt. "The wind doesn't blow on me, it blows right through me."

"That's what I wanted to show you," he said, and hand in hand, we went back inside. He sat cross-legged on the bed and I knelt again. It felt right. We stayed like that for a time. Then he said with a laugh, "A naked person can lie to another naked person. But it ain't easy."

I looked down at myself. I've never done that much. I hadn't liked or disliked my body until then. Somehow the attention I'd gotten from other people had always begun

with my face and my way of . . . oh, whatever my way was
. . . and drifted away before it got to my body. So I'd kept
it clean and covered up and had come to forget about it the
way everyone else did.

"It's a good one," Godbody said gently. He had a way of
knowing what you were saying deep inside yourself and
talking with it. Mr. Currier had the same sort of knack, but
he talked *to* it. "It's good just because it's a real woman's
body. Women's bodies," he said with total modesty, speaking out of his own really superb body, "women's bodies are
good-er than men's, just for openers, and then yours is a
good one of them." If I had said an eye-batting "thank you"
to that, I'd have wanted to wash out my mouth with soap.
So I said nothing but looked down at my body again and
touched it, on one breast and on my hip. I have never been
so pleased in all my life.

"Then what is it?" Godbody asked me after a time.

I looked at him, waiting so easily and patiently, and suddenly I was in a room in a house in a town in a world. "Oh."
And I didn't know where to begin.

Godbody said, "Everything's part of everything else,
Melissa. Begin anywhere."

"I'm leaving."

All right, a beginning. Did you ever talk to someone who
simply and totally listens? Do you know how rare that is?
Haven't you ever realized that nobody wants to listen except to get ready for the next thing they're going to say, or
to catch their breath, or to get ammunition from you for
their next sentence? Most of us want the listener to say
"uh-huh" and "yes" all the time, too, to tell us they're still
listening. But suppose you know someone is listening, and
he knows you know it, so he never says "uh-huh" or "yes."
It puts you into yourself in a way you've never known before. If you come to a place where you can't go on for a

while, he'll wait. He's not afraid of silence, and sometimes that can be very disturbing. So I talked, and Godbody listened to me.

"There's a man in town, they call him Hobo. He works night shifts in the coil-winding place in town, four to twelve, so he's kind of around all the time. There's a woman called Mrs. Mayhew, she owns a newspaper. She watches everything and everybody. There's a Mr. Merriweather at the bank, and he does, too. The one thing the two of them can't watch is the underside, the dirty part where Hobo lives. He knows everything there. Mrs. Mayhew knows some things about Hobo, and she hangs that over his head and he has to do what she wants. I've been typing in the newspaper office for Mrs. Mayhew."

I had to stop there for a bit to be sure I had all the pieces out in plain sight. I didn't want to say a lot about how I felt about these people or the things they did. I just wanted to say what happened. Feelings could come later.

"You can't work in a place like that with people like that without finding out what they are and what they're doing. I mean what they're really doing—not putting out a paper or running a bank or scoring with girls in the sickest possible way, but pulling secret strings and watching people jump a long way off, and having power over everything and everybody in the town. The way they use the power mostly is to stop anything from changing and to stop anything that could be fun or loving, and to fight anything that's beautiful or young just for that reason alone—that's the worst thing, that really is the enemy.

"So I found out . . . more than I wanted to. Believe me, it was much more than I wanted to and I tried for the longest time not to notice, and then not to let any of it matter. And I don't think I really realized until today why it was that she—

"Oh, but I've got to go back and tell about Hobo. Hobo is kind of slick-looking and swaggers around, and there's a lot of talk about him. I mean 'nice' girls don't go out with him, and some girls think he's dangerous—which he is— and stay away from him because of it, and some girls get right in his path or even chase after him because of it.

"I didn't do either one. I knew a lot about him—more than he knew I knew—but when he stopped me on the street and was nice to me . . . oh, even to *notice* me was to be nice, you'd have to be me really to understand that. So I said I'd meet him later on down by the bridge. He said he had something to tell me, and he hinted that he was in some kind of trouble that I could help him with because of my job . . . oh, it doesn't matter what he said, it was easy, easy, easy for him. It was the first time in my whole life a man had ever said to meet him somewhere. Not even after school. Not even in the high-school cafeteria for a forty-five-minute lunch.

"It was dark down there—he must have known it would be a dark night with the moon rising late, and at first I thought he hadn't come, that it was a cruel joke. And I blamed myself for that, not him—can you understand that? —because he talked with me on the street and made me laugh. So when I heard him call my name I could have cried with joy. Relief.

"I made it so easy for him!

"He was down off the road, on the riverbank, almost under the bridge. He said to come down and I did. I tore one of my stockings at the knee, and I remember thinking at first that that was a disaster and then being glad that it was so dark, surely he wouldn't see.

"There—you see? I began that meeting as one who could care about a torn stocking. I ended with—oh . . . "

This was one of the times Godbody waited without

speaking, as if he was listening to my silences as he listened to my words. He watched me the same way, speaking or not, receiving. It was during this silence that I wrestled with the problem of words. The words I would have to use if I told him everything. I knew I could hint and talk around and suggest, and I knew I could be very clear and exact with what are called "decent" words, and I knew I could say none of it and sprinkle the story with "you-knows" and "his thing" and "doing *it,*" but I couldn't, not with Godbody. He would listen and perhaps he wouldn't mind one way or the other—but I would. I would because he was Godbody, and because I was naked with him. I understood, in that quiet time, something I had heard Mr. Currier say once in a sermon: "Words have meanings—words mean things. There are a lot of things to be afraid of, and that's all right, but don't ever be afraid of a word." I was afraid of nothing, here with Godbody, least of all words. I went on telling him.

"I got down to the riverbank, and I couldn't see him. I couldn't see anything. I called out quietly, 'Where are you?' and his voice said, 'Right here.' I looked into black shadows, right, left. 'I can't see you.'

" 'Yes you can. Have a look,' and it was like lightning, a sudden glare of light so bright I screamed. The light was a patch maybe a yard off the ground, but it was too bright and sudden and too brief for me to make anything out.

" 'Know what that is?' It was Hobo all right, but this was not the voice that had made me laugh, made me meet him here. It was different. Rough, like pain or anger. I closed my eyes hard and studied the after-image still fading behind my lids. Something vague, soft, somehow convoluted, yellow-peach.

" 'I don't know.' I really didn't. I said, 'Hobo, what was it? Where are you?'

" 'I'll give you another look at it then,' he said from

somewhere, and again the light came. This time it stayed a little, and I realized it was a big flashlight and he was shining it on his penis. He had his pants all the way open and the penis and testicles hanging out. It looked very big and soft and it hung down and swung back and forth a little. I think he was turning his hips to make it do that. 'Now do you know what it is?'

" 'It's your pay-nis,' is what I said. I had never seen one before except on pictures and statues. I had never had occasion to use the word, and nobody had ever spoken it aloud to me as far as I could remember, so I pronounced it the way I had learned in school to pronounce Latin words.

"He said roughly, 'It's my cock, and I'm going to fuck you with it, you dumb cunt.'

" 'Hobo—don't!'

" 'Hobo don't,' he mimicked me, and the patch of light moved a pace closer to me; then angrily, 'Are you telling me what to do?'

"I didn't want him angry. I said, 'No, oh no. I mean don't keep that light on, someone will see.'

"He turned the light off. 'All right, you're not so dumb, you're just a cunt.'

" 'What's a cunt?'

"My eyes were still dazzled from the light, and the after-image was much clearer and more upsetting. I had no idea he had moved closer until I felt his hand roughly between my legs. 'That's your cunt.'

"I remembered then that I had heard that, somewhere. I said, I guess a bit stupidly, 'Oh, that's right. My mother used to call it my peewee.'

"He said, 'Oh, good Christ. Peewee. You're too goddam much, Melissa.''

"I said, 'Hobo, let's go someplace else. I don't like it here.'

" 'I like it here.' Angry again. Oh, I didn't want him angry. I said quickly, 'All right. All right, Hobo. We can stay here. . . . What do you want?'

"That's when he said it, the thing that made all the difference, the words that even now, when I understand so much better, still come back to me and give me a glimmer of that great choking explosion of joy. He didn't say it gently and he didn't say it with any warmth at all, but he said it, he said it. He said, 'I want you.'

"How can I ever find words to tell you how much that meant, coming that way, so unexpectedly, words so far remote from anything I ever thought I'd hear? I know I'm not too bright and I guess I was so terribly hungry to hear that, or something like that, from someone, anyone, that everything else in the whole world just dropped away and became less important. I said, I guess I sang, 'Hobo, oh Hobo, you do? You really do? Oh, tell me how, tell me what you want me to do!'

"I know how crazy that sounds, sitting here telling it. I wouldn't expect anyone to believe it. But this was me, you see, *me*. And that's what I said. And I reached out for him.

" 'Get your goddam hands off me.' I heard him jump back. I heard him breathing. My eyes were beginning to let me see one dark thing from another. I saw where he was and moved closer. He moved back, stumbled. He cursed, some word I didn't know and can't remember now. 'Keep away.'

"I thought I was doing it all wrong. I said, 'I'm sorry, oh, I'm sorry, Hobo. Tell me what you want me to do. Please.'

" 'Really too fucking much,' I heard him murmur; I think he was talking to himself. He asked me suddenly, 'Are you scared?'

"I tried hard to tell him the truth because I didn't want to lie to him, not in any way. But I was afraid of making him angry again, so I said, 'Yes I am, Hobo. Awful scared. I never did anything like this before.' And then quickly, quickly, 'But it's all right, it's really and truly all right, I won't run away, I'll do anything you say. Anything.' I began to cry.

" 'Oh, shit,' he said. Not to me, I think; to the night around him. I said, when I could, 'Let me help you, Hobo. Please let me help you.'

"His voice was angry again, angry and suspicious, and I could have died. I just couldn't do anything right. *What makes you think I need help?*' He barked it, and from the little I could see, I think he was going to hit me. I was going to duck away, but I fought that and won, too, and stayed where I was.

" 'You said you did. This afternoon.'

"That seemed right. I didn't know why. Anyway it made him slump back again. He muttered, 'Oh, that.' And that's when he jumped on me. Just then, without any warning of any kind. He came at me out of the darkness, diving like a football player, and knocked me right over. It hurt—my shoulder, my elbow. He held me down with a forearm across my throat and with his other hand he began clawing at my panty-girdle. I don't know why I'd worn the panty-girdle that night. I guess I thought I might look a little nicer in it. It fits very tight and it's a good one, mostly nylon with panels at the sides that stretch a little but not much stretch at all on the leg hems. He tried to tear it, and it just wouldn't tear. He tried to get his hand up inside, and there just wasn't room. I cried out 'Oh, wait, don't, don't, Hobo —wait!' and somehow that made him make a soft growling, grunting noise and try twice as hard, but it just wasn't any good. *Will* you wait!' I yelled in a flash of irritation I didn't know I could ever feel, and I kind of flipped myself, my whole body. I guess it caught him off balance or something. We were on the edge of a steep place on the bank and there was a flash of agony as his weight came on the forearm across my throat, but only a flash; he rolled right off me and down and away. I scrambled to my feet panting and pulled up my skirt and hooked my thumbs on the waistband of the panty-girdle and skinned out of it as if it was two sizes too large. That's when I lost my sandal, I guess. Hobo came scrambling up the slope, and I was able to see his hand thrust out, and I put the girdle into it and said, 'There! There, you see? You didn't have to do that. You just had to ask me!'

"He stood very still for a little while, breathing hard, and then he passed the girdle from one hand to the other and just dropped it on the ground. He sat down where he was and put his head in his hands. I knelt down next to him. I was afraid to touch him. After a long time I spoke his name softly. 'Shut up,' he said.

"But I wouldn't. I was much too upset. I pleaded with him. I said, 'If you really want me—I'm here. You don't have to force me. I guess you think I'm just awful, but I don't care, I'm telling you the truth. I know I'm doing everything wrong, but it's all so new, and if you'll only tell me what to do . . . '

"He growled at me, 'You have really fucked it up.'

"I didn't understand that and said so. And I said, 'All you've done this whole time is shout and grumble and act rough, and you just don't need to, Hobo! Why don't you just tell me what's *wrong?*' I thought I was going to cry again, but he startled me so much I guess I forgot to. He grabbed my wrist and turned himself around, sitting with his legs wide apart. 'Here, put your hand on it.'

"He put my hand on his penis. He almost shouted, 'Grab hold, don't just touch it.' I said, trying to gentle him, 'All right, Hobo,' and took hold of it. It was very big, I could barely get my hand around it, and it was soft, soft as new-baked bread wrapped in silk. 'Now do you understand?' he cried hoarsely and flung my hand away.

"It came to me then that Hobo Wellen was in some kind of anguish, and I'd have given away anything—my soul, if I have one—to know what it meant, to be able to do something for him. I had to say the truth, 'No, I don't understand. I'm sorry as I can be, Hobo, but I just don't.'

"I think there was real hate in his voice then, and oh, that hurt. 'You just got to hear it in so many words, don't you? You just want to hear me say it and laugh at me.'

" 'Laugh!' I was horrified by the idea, and I do think he believed me. He said, in simpleton-simple words, 'I can't get it up. It don't get hard. I can't do a fucking thing with it with you. Now I said it, so laugh. And tell everybody, too!'

"So then I put my arms around him, not because I completely understood it all, because I didn't, but just because he was hurting so. He sat there frozen with tension for a moment and then slumped down into my arms, onto my lap, and began to cry. I never knew men cried—not like that. I guess it hurts them when they do it. I thought he was going to hurt his throat. I stroked his face in the dark. His cheeks were twisted up and knotted like leg-cramps, and his eyes were swirled down closed like healed scars, and his face was wet. I said a lot of words and things that weren't words, and kissed him a bit and stroked his hair, all the while not knowing, kiss by kiss, stroke by stroke, whether or not I was doing it wrong again.

"He began talking into my lap, so at first I didn't know what he was saying. ' . . . know what it's like, nobody knows what it's like, goddam lousy no-good prick won't work unless a chick is scared or I hurt 'er, put 'er down, cuss her mother-guts.' There was more mumbling I couldn't catch and something about 'balls bust open 'fore I could serve the first six months,' which I didn't understand, and then he writhed around to look up and was talking to me. 'You, you're a goddam turn-off. You can't help it but you are.'

" 'Tell me what to do!' I cried.

" 'You can't.'

" 'I can. I will. Anything!'

"And he cried out, almost the way I had, 'You can't! I got to take, you dumb bitch—take! How the hell can I take if you just lay there and give?'

"We were still for a time then, his head in my lap. I think something had exploded out of both of us and left us exhausted. Finally I said, 'I could pretend . . . '

"He said, 'Shit.'

"Then he shook his head angrily and sat up. 'I'll have sore balls for a week over this. God damn that Mayhew bitch.' And that's the remark I didn't understand until today.

"He was going to get up, he was going to leave me. 'Isn't there any way at all I can—'

" 'Not a damn thing. Short of knockin' you out and cold-cockin' you.'

" 'Then do it.'

"He couldn't believe me. 'You're crazy.'

" 'All right, I'm crazy. Hobo, I said *anything.* '

" 'Lost my flashlight,' he complained.

" 'What do you need the flashlight for?'

" 'I wouldn't want to hit you with a rock. I could get into trouble if you got hurt bad.'

"So we crawled around in the dark under the bridge looking for his flashlight. We found it at last—I found it, near where he had rolled off me that time. I brought it to him. 'Will it leave a mark?' 'Christ, no!' he said, 'You think I'm asking for trouble?' I asked him where he was going to hit me—on the head? He said, 'I guess back here,' and he touched me high on the back of the neck, to one side.

" 'All right,' I said and lifted my hair away from the place and turned sideways to him. 'Jesus, Jesus,' he said; it was like an angry sobbing. He held the flashlight—it was a big one—by the lens and hit me.

"There was a shower of stars and then the earth lying up against me—it was not like falling at all. I was face down, and he rolled me over and fell on me. He was gasping, 'You out?'

" 'No.' It was hard to talk and hard to say that, too, but I had to tell this man the truth.

"He took my hand and pulled it down to his penis. 'Grab ahold. Feel that?'

"I felt that all right. The shaft was . . . pulsing—no, that's not the word, because pulsing is an in-and-out, or larger-smaller kind of thing. This was larger-larger-larger in quick heartbeat surges, firmer, stiffer, harder. I thought hazily that this must be what he meant by getting it up. I suppose if I had not been so dazed I'd have been terrified of it, but I wasn't.

"He snatched it out of my hand and rammed it hard up between my legs. It was a bruising blow but not a penetrating one. I guess I'm just too small for a man to enter. One more thing I can't do right . . .

"He settled the big rounded tip against me and pushed. It hurt but it wouldn't go in. I could feel it suddenly begin to collapse, and he cried out in fury and took a handful of my hair and twisted my head to one side and hit me with the edge of his hand. I can't say clearly exactly what happened after that. I know it was big and hard again almost instantly, and Hobo mouthed some shrill soft curses and then moaned, and a lot of warm thick wetness happened all over my belly and thighs. He became limp-heavy on me, and I swirled away down into some place blacker than under any bridge.

"When I woke up the sky in the east was lightening with moonrise, and he was gone. I was cold and the wetness on me was clammy and . . . oogy, and my head and neck hurt a lot. I pulled my skirt up out of the way and sat up, and then I had to stay there until the world stopped going round and round me. I got up shakily, gathered the skirt high around my waist with one hand, and like a three-legged animal worked my way on two feet and a hand down the bank into the shallow black water. I stood in it up to my knees and splashed and washed myself as much as I could. It felt wonderful after the first shock.

"I walked home in the dark, carrying my one sandal. Nobody saw me. I thought nobody knew, but then Mrs. Mayhew found out. I really think she knew just by looking at me, just by the way I acted. I don't know how to act, you know.

"But it wasn't until this morning that I figured out the rest of it, the bad part. She, that Mrs. Mayhew, gave me her column to type and it was all about Mr. Currier's wife, it was filthy. And I'd seen Hobo coming out of the rectory earlier, and I'd seen him go into the newspaper office, and now this story . . . and suddenly I knew, I knew the whole pattern.

"She has something on Hobo—who knows what?—it could be a half-dozen things. I know some myself. And he's afraid of her. And she sends him to do rotten things, and if he can do them, she has somebody new to know something about, so she can use them.

"That one thing Hobo said, under the bridge—'God damn that Mayhew bitch'—when I was so much trouble for him . . . I don't know why, but that came crashing back into my head when I read her rotten column. And it all fell into place. *She* made him do it, *she* put Hobo onto me.

"What I lost—oh, what a loss . . . I guess to anybody else it wouldn't be so much, but to me . . . He said he wanted me. He said he wanted *me*. Well he didn't, and he would never even have talked to me out in the street if it weren't for her.

"And why? *Why?* . . . Because I worked for her, that's why. Because I couldn't help but find things out, more and more, and I couldn't help learning what she did with the things she found out—I couldn't help learning about *her.* So she had to be able to protect herself, she had to get something on me. And there's nothing, nothing, nothing in my life she can use against me, how could there be? Nothing, nobody ever happened to me! So—she made something happen, and now she has something she can use if ever I wake up to how much power I have over her.

"I can't fight her. I can't stay. All I can do is run. I told her I wouldn't type her filth any more and I ran away. I won't go back. I haven't got very much, I'm all alone, I'll just leave it all."

Godbody waited for a time. It had grown dark. We found ourselves looking at the chain-swung candle and the pattern of links thrown on the beams. I looked at his face and his body, so clear, so untroubled. He met my eyes and smiled. "Leave it all to go where, and do what?"

I thought about that and then said, "Do you know, I just don't *care!* For a while I don't want what I've been, and I don't care where I'm going. I'm—out of it, for now, anyway." I reached back and touched my skirt, folded on a three-legged stool. "It's all like those clothes, off me. I'm out."

"The story too."

"Story?" Oh . . . Hobo, Mayhew, the bridge. All told and done with, and here I was with it folded away, out of it. "Yes. Off my back. Now, for now anyway, I'm just . . . *being.* I like it."

"Just being," said Godbody, "is a good way to be."

We were quiet together for a good long time then. We were alone sometimes, wandering about in our heads, and following one another sometimes, like the moment I found myself watching his face as he traveled some passage purely his own, which resolved itself in a smile which was also his alone; and sometimes we shared the sleepy bleat of a baby goat or a nightbird or the simple candlelit fact of being together, and of being. We did not touch again.

And then there were voices.

I didn't know how rigid I'd gone until he spoke to me. The voices were coming closer, climbing the log steps, and Godbody saw into my mind and said, "You going to put it all back on?"

I looked at him and at the clothes. I shook my head.

People came in:

Britt Svenglund. She set down two heavy baskets, removed a string of beads made of drilled river stones, and lifted the long gown up and over and off. She had quite the most beautiful body I have ever seen. She went to Godbody where he sat on the bed and laid her right wrist on the side of his neck for a moment while their eyes met, and then turned to me. She repeated the strange touch, but with both wrists on the sides of my neck. Something flowed from skin to skin—extraordinary!—and I fell right into her eyes, and when she straightened and stepped back, the contact somehow was not broken.

Mr. Currier came in, carrying two heavy shopping bags, bending to get in the low doorway, and behind him was his wife. I love that woman. The sight they saw brought them to some sort of peak—you could see that—but it wasn't shock or disapproval. I had a sudden flash of a story I'd read, where people who had lived for three generations underground came out one night and for the first time saw the sun come up.

And behind them, someone else—quite the last person in all the world I expected or wanted to see anywhere again, but most especially not here. There was one tiny intense moment of total panic, when the three-legged stool back there in the shadows became the most important thing in all creation—a goal, a refuge, an absolute necessity—and I turned my head to find myself looking in Godbody's eyes, which with total attention asked me *Well?,* and if I had an answer, it was *It is well.* I sat back, and I smiled.

Andrew Merriweather

MY WIFE HAS A little poodle named Boo. Boo will hump any available outstretched arm or crossed leg. My wife, who is ever so genteel, says, "Oh, naughty, naughty Boo to do such a dirty thing!" Boo doesn't listen.

The other day I got fed up with Boo frantically humping my leg, so I hit him across the nose with the *Wall Street Journal* and suggested to my wife that she either let him out to take care of his natural urges or take him to a vet. She replied that it would be dangerous because "Boo is just a little little boy—so very young yet."

The dog is eight years old.

I get tired of watching television with a perpetual background of "Oh, naughty Boo. Oh, how dirty, Boo!" so sometimes I just get up and leave. If I happen to come back later, I can expect to see her absorbed in television, with Boo humping away at her crossed leg. Every so often she will look down and give the dog a maternal smile. It gives me the creeps. And if I go in she uncrosses her legs and says, "Oh, naughty Boo."

All of which is why I prefer the company of Willa Mayhew to that of my wife. Willa confines her hypocrisies to that syrupy little bird in her column and deals with me with her insanity wide open. Willa, I think, would rap Boo's nose for humping if she were alone with him but would encourage it if I were present. Demonstrations of evil are the breath of life to Willa Mayhew, and I am only too happy to encourage her in it.

Everything humanity has become and has produced goes back not to the arch and the wheel, but far earlier to the recognition of straight lines and flat surfaces. Where a human being is strictured he is channeled, and like water in a pipe, the smaller the diameter the greater the pressure. To say nothing of the control in direction . . . . To accuse me of being against the natural thing is to misunderstand me. I do happen to prefer a box hedge to a bougainvillea, because the latter can only diffuse itself while a box becomes more dense the more you cut it back, and will willingly accept training in any direction and still stay healthy. The choice of plants which thrive under discipline is the secret of business and of individual people as well.

I do not operate under rules-of-thumb, but if I did, I would deny a bank loan out-of-hand to anyone who is, on first meeting, what is called "warm" or (mistakenly) "human" or seductive or cheerfully ingratiating. Let such people grow like weeds on someone else's property. I surround myself with practices, people, activities, and plants which can be contained and directed. I pride myself that there exists no passion, no emotional circumstance, which can cloud my clear vision of its worth and my ability to find a direction for it.

All of which again brings me to Willa Mayhew and my pleasure in her company, for in me these things are learned things, the product of a long and arduous and purposeful effort. Willa was born with them or acquired them early. Her instant and complete comprehension of these verities never ceases to amaze me, and bears out my conviction that intuition is not a magical leap from premise to conclusion, but a form of superspeed computation in which the individually reasoned steps are passed too quickly to be retained in the memory—but passed, not bypassed.

She has her own reasons for doing what she does, and I

have mine for doing what I do to direct her. It is rather amazing how often our completely separate reasons call for the same action. For example: in the matter of the Rev. Currier, I have found the man intractable in a number of ways. True, he has increased attendance and therefore collections—as Trustee for the chuch's accounts I am well aware of that—but in some other matters his attitude is something less than could be desired.

The church owns a two acre lot on Hedgerow Street which has been, for nearly a century, a children's playground. The little it brings in in community goodwill is not enough to pay for its upkeep, whereas the construction of a two-story, sixteen-unit Sunset House—a residence for senior citizens—could bring in very substantial funds, church-owned and tax free. The tax-free status of such property is, I think, doomed in this country eventually, and it seems a matter of elementary wisdom to take advantage of it while the taking is good.

The Rev. Currier, however, is adamant on the subject, and without his approval the playground cannot be replaced. The issue is greater than it seems, however. I would like to see a less popular man, if I must, in that pulpit, if he could be better managed. The Rev. Currier can be swayed only by logic powerful enough to upset his convictions, and his hold on those is often harder than one might suspect. Mr. Currier, in sum, is just too hard to handle, and some mild scandal might be of assistance in moving him along to some parish where his gifts might be better appreciated, while his replacement would almost certainly be more reasonable. Men of Currier's ideological stubbornness are rare in the clergy—rare, indeed, everywhere else.

Willa Mayhew, on the other hand, has always had a deep instinctive dislike of the Curriers, I think because of the rather startling beauty of his wife Liza, which has always struck Willa as a calculated affront. It does not matter whether or not this makes any sense—it motivates her in quite the right direction, and I can only be pleased.

Her ingenuity and resourcefulness are a source of great enjoyment to me. Her carefully nurtured relations with the town constabulary, the Sheriff's Office, the State Police and the county and state C.I.D.'s make it quite possible for her to call a raid, small or large, at any time on anyone. She uses this power sparingly and well, and knows as well as anyone that a raid all by itself can accomplish a great deal even if no convictions result from it. And her stable of what I secretly call "operatives"—like the Harrisonbury woman and the Wellen creature, who can be made to jump when she snaps her fingers—is a real delight.

Interestingly enough, we have never compared notes on this matter of motivation. If I feel pressure should be applied at some vital spot in the quiet picturesque little town of ours, Willa always seems to be able to find the weak spot where pressure can be most effectively applied. More: she probably found the weak spot months ago and has it filed away ready for use at a moment's notice. The Svenglund woman, for example. I feel basically that she is a harmless eccentric and would have no objections to her hermiting out there on South Mountain forever, except for my knowledge that she holds clear title to the best deposit of road shale within miles of here. The only way to get that shale for the state-federal highway project, due through here not fifteen months from now, is to get her out of there, for her house is built right on top of it. Public opinion, of the Mayhew variety, can accomplish this more quickly and more cheaply than any other known method.

All these thoughts reeled through my mind in Food Mart, our local supermarket, when I glimpsed the Svenglund woman and the minister pushing a shopping cart through the aisles and talking avidly. I paused a moment to watch them, trying to see them through Willa Mayhew's eyes. In her mind the presence of a man with a woman—any man with any woman—is a coupling, with all that the term implies, and I remember thinking how splendid an arrangement like that, involving these two people, would be. Just think: a liaison between the minister and this shameless eccentric from South Mountain. A vision of her property populated by bulldozers and loading machines was superimposed on another of a nice new Sunset House on Hedgerow street, honoring its aged tenants while with pleasing frequency they broke their leases by dying off. Then regretfully I let the visions fade. Planning is one thing, wishful thinking another. A couple with evil knowledge does not engage in open conversation in a supermarket—especially not these two. Still . . . there must be a way to profit by some combination of their weaknesses. I had determined to discuss it with Willa, meanwhile still wishing there was something I could think of to do with them right now, when they solved the problem for me.

"Andy. Andy Merriweather!"

I approached them. In their cart were apples, cheese, black pumpernickel, some early plums, a five-pound bag of whole-wheat flour and some raw sugar. I wished fleetingly that they had bought beer. "Yes, Dan. Evening, Miss Svenglund."

"Andy, I'd like to talk to you. Do you have a few minutes?"

"Of course, Dan. What is it?"

They looked at each other quickly. Ah—it involved both of them.

"Not here. Could you come up to the house?" Ah, again. I detected the signs of the nontrivial.

"If it's important—certainly. Let me call my wife, and then I'll be with you."

"Andy, thank you. Thank you *very* much," he said earnestly, and if there is anything in the world that offends me more than an ankle-humping poodle, it is a preacher's earnestness. How I feel about what I have to put up with as a banker, vice chairman of the Vestry Board, and Church Trustee is known only to me and God. "Why don't you just go on up to my house? We'll follow in a few minutes," he said.

Ah, that "we." Ah, that quick decision without consulting the Svenglund woman, meaning an understanding between them. Ah. "See you soon, then."

Outside the double glass doors of the market there is a phone booth, and it was in use. There is a technique for handling this situation, involving jingling coins impatiently in front of the caller, starting away and turning back and so on. There is another technique, however, when one feels concern about the caller and his messages, which involves leaning back against the wall beside the booth where he cannot see you and looking carefully away, so that the world sees your studied disinterest while your ear is aimed at the imperfect soundproofing.

The man in the booth was Hobo Wellen, looking as if he had been decanted from a concrete mixer full of rock dust, and he was so angry that he was yelling.

"No, I ain't going to tell you any more right now. All I want you to know is I saw him myself, a big redheaded guy. Just who and where and how, I'll say in my own time, so let's you and me be real nice to each other until then." He slammed out of the booth and ran blindly right past me, out into the parking lot.

The conjectures possible in the face of evidence like this were so numerous that I simply set them all aside, content to memorize what I had heard and file it away in my "Future Use" compartment. I was tempted to play with it: Who would Hobo Wellen be promising part of a story to, for example, and why was he so angry, and why was he raising his price? (For that "be real nice to each other" would be a treasure to him.) And finally, what was his story about a "big redheaded guy?" . . . It pleased me to be able to set it all aside for now, so certain was I that I could have the whole story virtually at will. I called home.

"Don't wait dinner for me," I said when she gave me the genteel Hello. "Church business." I then held the receiver away from my ear until I heard a pause, with a rising inflection: question. I said, "I didn't get that last."

She demanded, "Did you get Boo's din-din?"

Now if a preacher's earnestness is irritation, baby-talk is absolutely infuriating. "I did not," I said.

"But I asked you to, and you said you were going to the market."

"I am not," I said, looking up at the market's huge pillared sign, "going to the market." I do not lie.

"Then what about poor Boo's din-din?" she wailed genteelly. With some years of practice this becomes possible. I said reasonably, "Give him *my* din-din."

Immune to sarcasm, she cried, "Oh, but that might make him sick!"

"Yes," I said, "it might," and hung up. I got my car and drove to the rectory. Liza Currier let me in.

"Andy, how nice!" It startled me. She always welcomed me because she always welcomed virtually everybody—part of her job. But this was different. It couldn't have been anything about me that produced this warmth and sparkle —this is not modesty, but cold pragmatism—so it must be something that had happened to her. I wondered what would happen to the warmth and sparkle when next week's paper came out. I wondered, too, watching her stride as she ushered me into the living room, what life would be like with a woman like this as part of the daily—and nightly—

environment instead of the well-bred bundle of inanities I had selected as my life's partner.

A strange—for me, very strange—thought occurred to me as I followed Liza Currier those few steps from the door to the living room: that the boundaries of my wife's being were her clothes, but that Liza's body began inside her garments . . . that my wife seemed to be, through and through, weavings and stitches and seams and cloth; no bones, no flesh, no veins, intestines, organs; just factory-finished preshrunk moisture-retardant, man-made or totally processed fibers; whereas Liza Currier wore clothes the way the earth wears weather, and they really began at her skin, beneath which she was actual warm flesh and blood.

Mind you, I was not making a qualitative comparison; I was not saying that to be like Liza was a better way to be. If naturalness is better, then perhaps we should never have left the trees and the caves. Liza would be totally unsuited to the position in my life in which I had placed my wife. I had chosen a wife to be what my wife had become, and I felt no need to criticize my own decisions. Yet . . . there was a difference between the two, and it emerged rather vividly in the few seconds during which I watched Liza Currier walking. I said, "Dan's at the market and on his way back here with Britt Svenglund."

"Oh," she said, "How nice. Isn't she beautiful?"

"Is she?" This was a response, not a question; Liza did not attempt to answer it. I sat down in the not-quite-expensive, not-quite-worn wing chair supplied its pastor by the congregation, and she excused herself and flew into the kitchen.

Thoughts of my wife returned to me. Comparisons are not odious, as the old saw has it: comparisons are comparisons. My wife approaches the kitchen sedately and on time.

Over the years she has developed (at my suggestion and insistence) a basic collection of eight dinner menus. There are eight because there are seven days in a week, and therefore one does not have, say, chicken on successive Tuesdays. Arranged this way, meals are anticipated, but not monotonous; shopping is not subject to impulse buying; food preparation becomes increasingly expert (although I must say my wife's skill in overcooking a lamb roast has reached an unimproveable peak of tastelessness), and the appearance of leftovers in the refrigerator is absolutely predictable, which takes care of her lunches during the week and mine on weekends. So . . . never does she "fly" into the kitchen.

She is, I suppose, like the emu and the cassowary, a flightless bird in all respects. Flights of language, flights of imagination, and certainly flights of passion are quite alien to her and always have been. I met her when I was a teller at the First National Bank, and she impressed me in a number of ways. Not especially talented in anything, she had applied herself diligently in high school and for a year in business college, supporting a most creditable record purely on the ability to do exactly as she was told and absolutely nothing else. She was punctual and neat and had the admirable ability to listen attentively and talk very little. When I gained my assistant managership and was to be transferred here, and had carefully assessed the advantages of being married in a community such as ours, we became engaged one evening in an inexpensive restaurant and, after a suitable interval, were married. We had planned to go to Atlantic City or Niagara Falls for three days, but when I was offered the opportunity of attending an interbank conference on teletype credit procedures, I took her to Poughkeepsie, New York. She waited in the hotel room armed with some magazines and the Gideon Bible while I attended the sessions, and after a quiet dinner in the hotel restaurant we retired to our separate beds. I felt it premature to introduce her to all the facets of marriage at once, so the occasion passed very peacefully. And a good thing, too: twice she had fits of depression and crying at night, which was certainly no time to upset her with unseemly advances.

Inevitably, of course, these matters had to be included in our relationship. It was, after all, a marriage. We were both extremely young—I had not yet reached my mid-thirties— and I handled it the way I have handled any new enterprise: learn all one can, consult the experts, and then proceed with caution. I read everything I could find on the subject, which in those days was not very much. Some of this, of course, could be discarded at the first glance—the works of Havelock Ellis, for example, I regard as nothing but pornography. Poetic pornography, I will grant, but pornography nonetheless. Dr. Willey's heavy volume I found too clinical, too explicit, and almost devoid of moral values, while his profuse illustrations obscured their information in (for me) clouds of embarrassment. Dr. Stopes was more to my liking, and I patterned my approach on her advice, except for her assertion that the wife should possess all this information as well as the husband. I firmly believe that any man who permits his wife to know as much as he does about anything is a fool.

But as always caution prevailed, and before initiating these practices I sent my wife to Dr. Krebs (now deceased) to be fitted with a diaphragm. Not that I was particularly modern-minded in such matters. I just feel that everything should be planned.

Dr. Krebs was an aging German with an accent just thick enough to make him seem cultivated and to conceal a view of things I can only describe as coarse. "Anty," he said with a ribald gleam in his eye, after he had sent my wife out of his examining room and called me in, "Anty—" (there was, I think, something offensive in the way he used my nickname) "dere is somesing vitch hass to be done zat if I do it wiss my instruments it iss a sin against God."

I stood right up to him. "Don't be irreverent, Doctor. What has to be done?"

"Ze t'ing you haff to do mit *your* instrument, *dumkopf.* She hass a regrettable condition which needs correction. She iss a virgin."

I very much disliked his expression of suppressed laughter. This was a serious matter. I asked him how to proceed under the circumstances, and he became quite inarticulate. It was some time before I could explain to him that it was not the basic procedure I wished to discuss but only the matter of contraception. He was then able to tell me what to ask for at the drug store. I wrote it down in my notebook and took my wife home.

The next day I drove to a neighboring town and bought the prophylactics. They came three to a box. That night after dinner I told my wife that I would sleep in her bed. She colored violently and bowed her head. I think she misunderstood me because, after having given her sufficient time to get ready, I entered the bedroom and fumbled across the dark room to her bed only to find it empty. Taking me at my word, she had taken my bed. As things turned out, this was by far the best thing that could have happened, because I had had a series of misadventures in the bathroom while preparing myself. On opening the little box I had bought at that distant drugstore, I found three rather surprisingly long, limp rubber sheaths, but no leaflet of instructions of any kind. A serious oversight of the manufacturers. I understood, of course, the principle of the things, but the knack of stuffing a small limp male organ into one of them was beyond me. The first one I broke with my thumbnail. The dry rubber against my dry skin was recalcitrant. The second one I lubricated inside with soapy water. It slid on easily but fell off as soon as I stood up. By this time my manipulations had brought about a local excitement which disturbed me very much. I had been taught early that excessive handling of the genitals was dangerous to the mind and soul, and was to be avoided at all costs. I took immediate measures: a cold shower, which took so long to bring about a normal relaxation of the organ that I caught quite a chill. I then put on the third sheath, having struck the right degree of lubrication by having it wet but not soapy. It was much longer than it needed to be and it was necessary for me to hold it in place with one hand the whole time I was getting into my pajamas, but I succeeded. Under the circumstances, finding her bed unoccupied was a rather welcome surprise.

It was almost a week later that I had another opportunity to go out of town and return to that pharmacy, where I asked to see the pharmacist in his back room and lodged a complaint. The idiot kept saying, "What? What?" and looking at me strangely, but I persisted, and he sold me another brand which, he said, were ready-rolled and would give me no trouble. I returned home with them and found them much more satisfactory. I performed my marital duty as quickly and as forcefully as I could. I had no intention of being forceful, but it turned out to be much more difficult than I had thought. At first it seemed absolutely impossible to penetrate her, and I think I became a little angry. When the tissues yielded she screamed and after that cried a good deal, but anyway it was done, and I went back to bed satisfied, at least in my mind. The animal part of me satisfied itself during the night, which quite disgusted me. All in all, it was not a pleasant experience, and I understood the wisdom of the Creator who associated these organs so closely with the other disgusting functions. When I tried to explain this point to my wife at breakfast she said, "You didn't even kiss me," and burst into tears, a non sequitur which forced me out of the house without my second cup of coffee and put my whole day out of step.

In due course Dr. Krebs completed his fitting—without the pleasure of my company, you may be sure—and in another week the diaphragm arrived in the mail. This, I learned (much later) looked like one of the second lot of prophylactics I had bought, all rolled up, but about five times as large. The rubber rim concealed a coil spring, and there were, unlike the male's devices, voluminous instructions on preparation, insertion, removal, cleaning and maintenance. My wife is, as I have mentioned, an expert on doing exactly as she is told, and I was certain that she could manage these rituals quite handily. My surprise and irritation is therefore understandable, I think, when the appointed occasion arrived and I awaited her in the bedroom, and she came in, turned on the light and sat down on the edge of her bed with a woebegone, frightened and embarrassed expression on her face. She held like a scepter in her hand what looked like an oversized blue plastic toothbrush handle, minus the bristles and bearing a small spur partway down and, at the tip, two blunt prongs.

"What," I demanded, "is that?"

She looked at it as if she had forgotten she had it and quickly and uselessly tried to hide it behind her back. She was then forced to explain that it was an insertion device for those of such delicate sensibilities that they could not bring themselves to touch that area of their bodies with their hands, which I can certainly understand.

It was not easy to get a coherent explanation from her beyond "It's *gone*, Andy. I can't *find* it," to which I responded with some asperity that she wasn't supposed to find it until afterward. She then explained to me that I didn't understand; it was not where I evidently thought it was. It seemed that she had not been able to insert it at all, and now it was *"gone,* Andy. I can't *find* it!"

Further discussion brought some tears and, from me, a good many get-to-the-points and, at last, an account of what had happened. Given several alternate choices of postures to assume in performing this act, she had chosen to lie on her back in the dry bathtub with her knees raised and separated. The diaphragm, well anointed with a jelly that came with it, was to be stretched from the two prongs at the tip of the applicator and hooked to the spur below. According to the instructions it could then be inserted to the correct depth, where a slight rotation of the applicator would disengage the object from its position on the handle and it would then snap in place internally.

She did everything properly up to the point where she was ready to insert the contraption. She lay back in the tub, and the instant her eyes came off what she held in her hand, there was a sound . . .

During the subsequent discussion and search I forced her to reproduce that sound. It was the only clue we had.

. . . like *phutphooPLOP.* She raised her head to identify it and found her scepter empty of the rubber device. Puzzled, she rose out of the tub and began searching. She searched everywhere in that bathroom, getting down on her hands and knees, even going prone on the cold tiles to look under the tub. At last in despair she had come to me for assistance, still blindly carrying her fairy wand.

When at last I had absorbed the situation, I got out of my bed, and into my slippers and robe, and gave her what I am sure was an eloquently scornful look. I stamped into the bathroom while she tiptoed timorously after me.

A quick glance around failed to produce an instant discovery. I glared at her again and moved the shower curtains and stooped and peered and shifted. I then descended to my knees and, on them, walked painfully around that bathroom searching. Ultimately, I was flat on my stomach peering under the tub.

Nothing.

I sat on the floor and looked up at her. "Why couldn't you have been just a little bit careful?" I demanded. She wailed that she had so been careful. It was at this point that I had her keep trying to reproduce that sound until she was satisfied that it was right. I tried it until we were both satisfied that I had it down properly. *PhutphooPLOP*, we said to each other. *PhutphooPLOP*. I then began to analyze the sound.

Phut we agreed was the sound of the spring-loaded diaphragm leaving the applicator. The *phoo* was rather more special. Unaspirated, it was more of a whir or silent whistle than anything else, and we agreed that it must have been the sound of it flying through the air. The *PLOP*, however, eluded us.

Disgusted and giving up at last, I shook my head and stood up, bringing my still shaking head up on the underside of the sink. I felt as if I had been most unjustly attacked and said an angry word to my wife, whose eyes were very round and most of whose knuckles were in her mouth. I then turned to assess the damage and found myself looking straight at the diaphragm, which, by suction and by its lining of viscous jelly, had adhered to the very center of the mirror.

"Here it is," I said, "as any fool can plainly see," and, with my dignity intact, I stalked out, leaving the silly woman to make up her mind what to do next. I went to my bed and in due course she went to hers, which, I suppose, was the only possible ending to the episode.

All of which, unaccountably, flickered through my mind

in the brief few minutes between Liza Currier's quick grace-
ful exit and the entrance of the minister and the Svenglund
creature.

"Andy, I really am grateful," Currier said, coming over
to me and quite unnecessarily shaking my hand. "Don't get
up." I wasn't getting up. "Britt—do sit down."

Britt. Ah! Not Miss Svenglund.

The woman, in her long robe, slid across the room as if
legless and on tracks, turned and settled on the divan. She
had not spoken a word to me in the market, and she did not
here. I wondered why.

Currier murmured something polite and left the room,
presumably to salute his wife. What I did on returning to
my home was to glance about out of the corner of my eye
to see if my wife was visible and if the evening paper was
on the end table. If so, I said, "Ah, the paper," and if not,
I sighed. Then I caught myself making comparisons again
and wondering why. I looked up and saw Britt Svenglund
looking at me.

I am not accustomed to being looked at in that way.
Women, I have discovered, do not look at me very much
at all unless they are about to speak. If I catch them at it,
they smile. Well, most people do. Most smiles are as un-
necessary as a preacher's handshake, and mean very little.
Even angry people smile. Most people smile even when you
turn them down for a loan. I have never been able to understand why, but they do.

Britt Svenglund did not.

The few people who do not persistently and vapidly
smile are either disinterested or mean to be offensive. Britt
Svenglund was neither. She looked at me levelly, with great
attention, and though there appeared to be no hostility in
her, I found the experience most disturbing. I shifted in my

chair and am sorry to say I smiled at her. I did not want to, and the effect must have been rather ghastly. After that I could do nothing but return her gaze.

I had seen her around town, every now and then, for years, but now I had to admit to myself that I had never *seen* her. She was markedly taller than I might have recollected, if indeed I had bothered to recollect her, and more full-bodied, and her face was stronger and more regular than I might have realized, the eyes larger and farther apart. Really, rather impressive.

Could Dan Currier be forming a liaison with this woman? I had the awful feeling that I was about to ask her, and that if I did she would tell me.

Rather to my relief the Curriers returned, with her hand in his while he said persuasively, "No, no, Liza—I want you in on this. It concerns you. Never mind the coffee." They seated themselves on the divan next to Britt Svenglund and joined their gazes to hers. I felt impaled.

"Andy—you spend considerable time with Willa May-hew. You must know more about how her mind works than anyone."

I said drily, "I never considered myself especially perceptive, Dan." The message was, I'm not going to help you, and I think he got it.

He leaned forward and grew intense. Oh, I do hate it when a minister gets intense. "Look, Andy, I'll level with you. I've discovered that Willa intends to print something about Liza in the paper next week, something pretty awful."

"About me!"

He took her hand, and I said carefully, "I don't think it's her practice to mention anyone, Dan. Not by name."

"No one ever doubts who she means, and you know it."

"What's she saying?" Liza asked.

"That you're—what's the term one uses?—entertaining men while I'm out on calls."

"Dan!"

"Sweetheart, I'm not concerned about what she says. I know it isn't true. I want to know why."

He was making that demand of me, and I was not comfortable. I said, "If it isn't true then there is nothing to be afraid of."

And then Dan Currier really surprised me. He said, "Andy, I want you to know first of all that I am not afraid of anything—not any more. Secondly, I have discovered that we don't live in a world where 'true' or 'not true' makes any real difference to people. We should, but we don't. It isn't whether or not a thing is so, it's what people say, and how they're made to say it, and most especially, why."

Again, but with a great difference, Liza cried, "Dan!" and when he looked at her, added, "I didn't know you knew that."

I hadn't known either. I looked at the minister and for the first time realized that he could after all be an angry man —more: that he was angry now. It is hard for me to put in words how deeply disturbing this was. There are things one knows and counts on: the laws of gravity and the cycle of seasons; Wellen is a sexual psychopath; there is money to be made from religious respectability; Daniel Currier is not a realist. On these things one builds one's structures, and using them, one manipulates things and people. Doubt any one of these, and it casts doubt on them all. I took refuge: I said nothing.

He pursued me. He spoke to me as he had never spoken before to me or, as far as I know, to anyone before. He made no attempt to be polite or to let me know (as he always had before) that perhaps I might be right for reasons that he was ignorant of, and in that case he was ready to listen. Gloves off, and most uncharacteristically (from what I knew of him) sure of himself, he laid it down.

"Andy, you run this town—you and Willa Mayhew. No— don't interrupt me! Don't give me a lecture about the town board and local ordinances and county and state laws and a regulated school district. You know what I mean. I am not going to discuss what motivates you; I just want you to know that I know what you are doing. I know too that you do whatever you can to strengthen the structure that exists —only because it exists and not because it is good. Only because you can use it, and the stronger it is, the stronger you are. You use the church for that, and the bank, and also you use Willa Mayhew and her newspaper.

"I don't think you are attacking Liza for any personal reason, or any simple reason either. It's more likely that you are attacking me. The reason you're doing it this way is that it's more effective this way. You see, I don't think you're a coward, Andy. Far from it. If a direct attack would work better, I'm sure you'd use one. So let me ask you straight: why are you attacking me?"

I liked none of this and said so. I stood up and said, "I don't have to stay here and listen to this." Whereupon the minister gave me my second surprise in this astonishing evening. He put both hands on my shoulders and said, "Oh, yes you do," and I found myself seated again so abruptly that I felt a tingling in the bridge of my nose. He is a very large man, and the weight of those two hands seemed to dissolve my knees and my jaw. I sat with my mouth open, looking up at him as he returned to his place and put his arm around his wife. She was as astonished, I think, as I, but unlike myself, she seemed to be full of joy. The Svenglund woman was looking at him too, and though her face was impassive still, her large eyes were very bright.

"The ques—," I began, but somehow my voice failed me. I swallowed, and there was nothing in my dry mouth to swallow. I cleared my throat. "The question is, uh, out of the question," I fumbled. "I have not seen Willa's column." My shocked brains began to work. "Neither have you— have you?"

He did not answer. He did the worst thing to me he could have done—said nothing, made no gesture, gave me nothing to use to change the subject. I said, "I don't pretend to understand Willa or what she does. I have no evidence that she is attacking anyone, but if she is, her reasons are her own. You should be asking her, not me." Again I waited, and again he waited me out. I began to be afraid of this man. "You have no evidence that I have ever attacked you. Have you?" Silence again. I yelled, "You can't prove it!"

"You can't deny it. You've just said a lot of things, Andy, but not once have you denied it. I know you—you do not lie. Can't you take that one small step that will make you tell the truth?"

I said, from the depths of my being, "I want to go home . . ."

"Oh God," Currier cried suddenly—and it came from him in a priest's voice, it was a priest's prayer: "Who can make this man tell the simple truth?"

And Britt Svenglund spoke up, spoke the only word I had heard from her in this insane encounter:

"Godbody," she said.

Harrison Salz

PICKED UP SPEEDER ON Winter Road by the bridge. It was Councilman Pruett, let him go. Stopped a couple kids hitchhiking. Homely girl, bad skin. Hassled them a little but no fun, they just took it. Kicked his ass. Got a kitten out of tree for old Mrs. Amplick. Give me a drink and five dollars. Think she smokes pot. Well, let her. Checked in 8:03, Chief wouldn't let me take the car home. That's that for night riding. The boys'll be sorry about that. Knockin around the back roads with a couple beers and a couple friends is livin.

Walkin home, car pulls up, someone calls me. I see the car is Hobo Wellen's shot-rod. Some day the top crust is going to quit coddlin Hobo Wellen, and he'll get his. Meanwhile you best listen, and sure enough, he's got Mrs. Mayhew in the back.

"Get in, Harry."

I get in but I say, "I got to—" and she says with that special honk in her voice, "You're coming with us," so I say "Well okay."

Nobody tells me nothin so I don't ask. Some day, boy. Some goddam day there won't nobody be able to "Get in Harry" me. Somebody wrote in the paper part-time constables got too much power. They should know. Half the people hate you, most of the rest laugh, you got to take every chance you can to show 'em who you are. You work when the Chief feels like it, and when he don't you don't, but boy you better be on call twenty-four hours anyway or else. Too much power. Boy.

I says, "Where we goin?" and Wellen says, "South Mountain," same time as Mrs. Mayhew says, "wait and see." I know who to listen to so I shut up again. My time will come, but it ain't come yet. Mrs. Mayhew, she had my number since I was on the force sixty days. How she found out about Denette I don't know. Night shift, summertime, just making the rounds, saw this Denette Francosi two o'clock in the morning out on the Ridge Road in her nightgown. In and out of her nightgown. Had only the one arm through it, the other side hangin down, the one tit out. Stopped. She come up past the car and begins to pass. Had to get out, she wouldn't answer. Caught up with her, grabbed her, she hangs on to me, starts to cry. Says she's sleepwalkin. Never even tries to cover up. Get her into the car, try gentlin her, get hot. Next thing she's tearin at me, gets it out, goes down on me. I come, she swallows the load. She squirms down on the back seat, I give her a good bangin and take her home. Very next mornin get a call to go down to the newspaper office to look at scratches on the door, was someone tryin to get in? Wasn't no scratches, was Mrs. Mayhew, she says it's time we got to know each other, she tells me about some town policeman stopped a girl two in the mornin sleepwalkin, made her do somethin unnatural (that's what she said), raped her, took her home. I didn't say nothin, but lookin at those serious crazy eyes of hers I knew she *knew,* she wasn't guessin. Got out of there, went and found Denette at the playground where she worked twice a week, cussed her out for tellin, she swore she never. Mrs. Mayhew all the time talks about a little bird sees everythin. I almost believe it. Unless she got somethin on Denette made her lie to me about tellin. Got to thinkin for awhile maybe even Mrs. Mayhew put her up to it but that's just too crazy. Ain't it? The next thing is old Ogilvie's accident, run off the high shoulder on the County Road, so drunk I took him home. Mrs. Mayhew stops me on the street to tell me next day she knows about the $18.50. I could swear Ogilvie was passed-out drunk and never seen a thing, so how did she know, how did she know how much? There was plenty left in his wallet, I ain't stupid. So either she got Ogilvie to act out the whole thing because she had somethin on him too, which nobody is goin to believe, or she really has got that little bird. I ain't afraid of no man alive, although I know when to keep my mouth shut and when to wait my chance, or no woman either, but I am afraid of that little bird.

So here we are goin through the intersection and up the dirt road and Wellen stops at the bridge over the dry creek. Mrs. Mayhew she honks at him, what does he think he's doin, move on up a piece and hide the car. "Oh, sorry," he says, and he's mad, and I think *you too?* I can imagine what the little bird seen him doin, he's a dirty kink, everybody knows that. We go on around the bend and Hobo stops and backs the car through a shallow ditch into the woods. We all get out and Mrs. Mayhew passes out flashlights to us and she has one too, then it comes to me it was not no accident she happened along when I got off shift, it probably wasn't no accident the Chief wouldn't let me take the car.

"Don't use the lights unless you have to," she tells us, and we come back down the road to the bridge and off the end and down the bank to the creek bed. "Oh," I says, "the squarehead," meaning the kook Skywegian broad that lives up here, nobody else does. She says, "Shut up, Harry," which sometimes is a thing I swear is wrote on my forehead and everybody I meet reads it off to me, shut up, Harry.

Well it was hard to shut up and not to use the lights, we all three done it and talked up too, mostly Ow and Shit and I will not stand for that language. That last is her. Because believe you me that is the roughest road in the dark you ever want to hit. Finally when we come to the steps the squarehead cut in the bank, do we walk up 'em? We do not. We do the mountain-goat bit up the other side, slippin and fallin and tryin not to cuss till we come to a flat place with burrs, thorns and somethin or other that makes my head itch an my eyes water, I don't know what, but anyway it's right across from the house. We get settled down and it's too far away for me to see, but Mrs. Mayhew, she unslings a big pair binoculars from a leather case and props 'em up. She's quiet a long time, so are we, then I hear her smackin her lips. Yes I mean smackin her lips. After a while Ahhh, she's sayin, ahhh, ahhh. It sounds like she's seein somethin good, but I know her and I heard that before, I was on raids with her, that Ahhhh means real bad trouble for somebody.

Hobo says, "Listen!" and I hear it too. Somebody's comin from the road, more'n one, more'n two . . . more'n that I can't say. Not tryin to be quiet neither, and they have a light.

"Harry," Mrs. Mayhew says, "quick nip over there by the house where you can see in and hear. I want to know everything. Every last thing, you understand that? Quick, before they get there. Don't be seen. There are people inside the house already. Jump!"

Oh never a please and never a do you mind, and what the hell is nippin and can you do that and jump too? Oh lady, some fuckin day . . . but I jumped or nipped or whatever and got my ass down the slope and across the creek and up the steps without nobody seein me but a baby goat I stepped on a little bit under that big wide eave she's got. I scrabbled back and around huntin till I found a place I could hunker down under an open window. I could hear real good, but I didn't want to put my head up. I felt around, and there right at the edge of a board the mill had sawed through a knot and it had fell out, and somebody, I guess the squarehead, had stuffed it full of what felt like moss with some sticky hard stuff in it—balsam, it smelt like. I got out my knife and worked at it careful, careful, doin it up and under so's the bits all fell out on my side. Real soon I had a pinprick of light in the hole, and then I slowed down a lot and gentled it all out. It was great. Best peephole I ever had on the job, I could sit on my ass to use it, yes and a peep show to go with it.

Bare-ass nekkid. That's the first thing hit me, wow. Bare-ass nekkid. And would you believe it, Melissa Franck. Holy Christ, and who would ever know she had a build like that. You go for the centerfold in girlie books, well fine, so do I, but you ain't never goin to see the likes of this there. Like she ain't thin, but anyone says she's fat is wrong. Like if you say she's big, you'd be wrong because she is not tall. I know the word I want to use, but I will not use it.

Then, the guy. Stranger. Better'n six foot, wide and flat. Redheaded with a long dong on him. They must of fucked already because they wasn't doin nothin, not even talkin. He was on a kind of bed thing in the corner, leanin back on one arm. She was kneelin on the floor next to him, like watchin his face. His face I could see pretty good by the one big candle swung from a chain. I never seen a face just like that one. You couldn't say how old. There's a kid in town fourteen has a face old like two hundred years, I don't mean wrinkled, but how he looks at you, what he knows. This guy was like that.

I seen a light, I heard some talk from the people comin, but I can't say who. I hunkered down and got flat against the boards to be sure they wouldn't see me, not that I had to worry, they'd of had to come right around to the side of the house and turned the light right on me and the door was up at the other end. When I was sure they had got there I heaved up and looked again.

First in was Britt Svenglund, my God, she reached down and lifted the long dress right off, and I always thought she didn't wear nothin under it and I was right. Oh Jesus God in heaven what a build on her. You don't see that kind in no centerfolds either but that's just because they can't get one. She goes straight to the redhead and does a funny thing, she puts her two wrists against the sides of his neck and looks into his eyes. If you should ever see anyone do that do you know what? You want to do it too. Then she goes to Melissa Franck and does the same thing.

Meanwhile who should come in the door loaded down with groceries but the minister, I mean Currier himself, and his little wife Liza. If this was goin to be the time I would see Liza Currier bare-ass it was goin to be a day to remember. There is not a guy in town under eighty that hasn't thought that one over. Oh, she is a dish. Currier puts down his bundles, and she moves close to him and they stand there lookin at those three nekkid people, and who should walk in the door then but Mister Merriweather the banker. He didn't come far. Soon as he seen those nekkid people he stopped dead, and the only reason he didn't turn around and walk out I think is he couldn't.

The minister started toward him and so did Britt Svenglund. Walked straight up to him, he didn't know where to look. She says, "You are welcome to this house." She says it in that funny squarehead way of talking she has. She says, "I would like you to understand about my house." She says, "If I were to come to your house I would obey your rules. Here in my house you may obey your rules too." Then she says, very serious: "But in my house you may not expect me to obey your rules. I will not do it. Now come in—truly you are welcome."

Mister Merriweather opens his mouth and starts to turn,

and Mr. Currier puts out a hand and turns him right back
again. The hand slides down to his arm, and he walks him
in. He is a big man, the minister is. Mister Merriweather
walks past Britt Svenglund nekkid and Melissa Franck nekkid, and I really don't think he is goin to make it. Mr.
Currier marches him to the redheaded man and turns him
loose. "Andy, this is Godbody."

Godbody stands up. He comes up so smooth it's like he's
growin fast and like he's not goin to stop. When he stops
he's lookin down and Mister Merriweather has to look up.
Godbody reaches out his two hands, and I do believe if Mr.
Currier wasn't standin there still he'd of bolted like a rabbit. Godbody lays his wrists against the sides of Mister
Merriweather's neck and holds them there.

Now I couldn't say this if I didn't happen to be just in the
right place and just then Britt Svenglund didn't light a
lantern in a bracket on the far wall so the light come across
Mister Merriweather's face. Mad-scared, just scared, slow
surprised. I got to tell you, he is surprised three different
ways onetwothree fast as that, you could see it happen, and
then he is hung in this Godbody's eyes like with fish-hooks
and leaders. Then when Godbody takes his hands off him
he all but drops. I mean his knees buckle.

He says, "Who are you?"

"Godbody. Who are you?"

Know what Mister Merriweather says then? He looks to
the right and to the left and I bet he sees nobody, nekkid
or not, and he says, "I don't know."

The squarehead takes hold of his hand like he was a
scared kid. She says, "Come, come," and leads him away,
but you know what, he backs away from that Godbody. I
mean I seen a movie one time, there is this king and nobody
leaves him walkin straight, they back out. It's like that.

"Come help me." She takes him to the far end by the door, it's fixed up like a kitchen, she begins takin stuff out of the bags and baskets.

The preacher stands there smilin down at Godbody while the redhead folds himself back down on the bed. "It's good to see you again, Godbody."

"Good to see you, Dan. Who is that?" The redhead points at Liza Currier. The preacher gets the funniest smile on his smile, if you can see what I mean. He waves her over where she's still standin, and she starts movin. "Why don't you ask her?"

I never hear people talk the way these people talk. I never seen people like these, neither. It has to be these people actin this way, anybody else and it would be just plain crazy. There's somethin happenin in there makes everythin right.

The naked man puts out his two hands and Liza Currier goes slowly down on her knees, lookin into his eyes, and he touches her too that way, wrists on her neck, and says, "Who are you?"

"Liza Currier." She whispers it.

Next to her Melissa Franck is kneelin too, but sittin back on her heels, and she's watchin all this, smilin like she knows somethin. Godbody takes away his hands and smiles at her. He says, "You sure are, Liza. You sure are." And next thing you know the reverend is down on his knees too. You don't know if this is just because the redhead is on the bed and the bed is low and there ain't no chairs or if it's . . . if it's—some other reason they kneel. I mean, I'm out there in the dark, peekin, and I am like spooked.

Currier is kneelin next to Melissa, and he says, "How is it now," and she turns her face away from Godbody and gives him such a smile I got to squinch up my eyes. She says it's all right now—it's all right. And he smiles back and reaches across and takes his wife's hand. He says to Melissa,

"This may be a strange thing coming from an ordained minister of Christ, but there once was a goddess who had many names—Cybele, Demeter, lots of others. In her earliest form she was known as the Great Mother of the Gods —she's about the oldest deity we know about.

"And if there ever was such a goddess, such a woman, she must have looked like you."

"Oh," Melissa says. "Oh. Oh." And that Godbody, he says a whole bookful with one word. "Hey . . . ," he says. And for a second I can't see what's going on because the whole scene melts and runs down my face. God damn it. You see what I mean. It was weird. I am sittin there wipin my eyes because the preacher used the word I was afraid to use even inside my head.

Britt Svenglund has one hell of a big wooden bowl, somebody must of burned a big tree stump to hollow it out, then cut it away and scraped it, I don't see how else you could make such a thing without you got a turret lathe. She had it piled full of fruits and nuts, stacked just so and so, with all the colors fixed to show, and there was other things in it, black bread cut in rounds and diamond shapes with white homemade butter spread on it, and flowers too, here and there, and there was a couple of those dried Indian gourds from last fall, with all the colors and warts and funny shapes, and early berries. I don't know nothin about flower arranging, but some people do and there is whole clubs about that, and books too, so there must be somethin to it, and this Britt Svenglund she has it all down. That bowl, it sure was pretty. So anyway she's got these big stone or clay platters with bowls of sour cream and butter, and five, six kinds of cheese, and apple slices, and a couple stone jugs, I guess milk and cider, and she brings them to the place by the bed where everybody is kneelin, and she goes back and reaches for the bowl, and like I said, it is a big bastard of a bowl. And what do you know but Mister Merriweather takes it away from her. She is probably twice as strong as that dried-up moneychanger, but the way he does it she kind of curtsies. You never seen a nekkid woman curtsy. Well, she did, and he come on down the place slow and careful like in the movies with organ music, one of those the-king-of-Russia-gettin-married things. Mister Merri- weather.

And everybody moves over and moves back and he sets the bowl down on the floor, a lot of hands comin up to help as he lowers it down or else he just has to drop it, he ain't picked up anythin heavier'n a mortgage form for twenty years. And he kneels down. Maybe after totin that bowl he had to, I dunno. And then Liza Currier—

Oh Jesus and then Liza Currier drops her husband's hand and puts her two hands down, crossin her arms, takin the edge of the pullover in her hands, and she gives him such a beggin look like I never saw. He hangs in there for a long time lookin at her and then he says, "Liza darling, of course!" like they are mindreadin or some such, and I got to stop breathin as she whips the sweater up and off over her head, and stands up and kicks off her sandals and drops her skirt, and she got no underwear and any woman put together small and solid like that don't need it, oh Jesus, there isn't nothin more perfect than that little woman, she got tits much bigger'n you suppose and almost no hair on her pussy, more like soft shadow you can see the pink meat through. All that, but I got to say too you can't talk dirty about that once you see it bare. I mean, you can long as you work it up in your head, but once it's there it's so goddamn perfect the dirt falls off. Oh, shit, I don't know what I mean.

And everybody watchin looks glad but not hard-on glad. And they all look at Godbody, and he stretches out his hands over the big bowl of fruit and flowers and he says thank-you for this. I think then he is goin to reach for some of it when he sits straight up and holds up the one hand like a traffic cop, and everybody stops talkin, breathin too, I guess. Godbody says, "There's someone outside."

Well I was in the service and I done a stretch in jail once which nobody knows but Mrs. Mayhew and I been on the force a year and a half or better and I seen a lot and I never yet chickened out, but this time I damn near. And it wasn't just gettin caught, which always makes a man feel like a fuckin moron, and it wasn't what they might do to me in there because when you get right down to it there wasn't nothin much to be scared of except maybe that Godbody . . . about him you just couldn't tell, he wasn't like nobody else I ever seen. It was somethin else. There was somethin happenin in there that had not happened yet if you see what I mean, and if this stopped it I wouldn't get to see it. And maybe I thought if this stopped, it would be a goddam shame.

Anyway I quit breathin and hung my eye in that hole mostly because I couldn't move. Godbody and the preacher was on their feet and out the door like they was yanked by the same string. I drop down in the angle between the house and the dirt and press myself into it, wishin there was mole in my family tree. It is dark and I'm scared and somehow mad at myself and someone comes skiddin round the corner and all but steps on me an kicks a spray of gravel in my face and then there's an *Ooof!* and a squealin like a stuck hog, one long squeal, and a lot of breathin and stampin and there I am layin there tryin to believe that the whole thing is done and it's got nothin to do with me. And I got to believe it because it's so, and I get my eye back to the hole.

And here comes Godbody and Mr. Currier and in between them, glassy-eyed and spit on his chin, is the scared-est Hobo Wellen I ever did see, throwin his head side to side an makin little bits of that squealin noise.

Melissa Franck, she jumps up and runs over there callin, "Hobo, Hobo," and tries to put her hands on him. God-body says real quiet, "Let me, Melissa," and turns loose of Hobo. Mr. Currier keeps a hold, I don't think to trap him, I think to hold him up. Godbody takes Hobo Wellen by the chin and turns his face up. Wellen is whimperin like a cur-dog and his eyes is rollin. Godbody just holds his chin so's his head can't move and looks into his eyes and those eyes slow down and pretty soon stop, they're lookin back at Godbody. Godbody makes a wave with his free hand *go back,* and Mr. Currier lets go of Hobo and steps out of the way. Godbody lets go of Hobo's chin. Now here was a man scared right out of his mind, it took two big men to catch him and hold him, but now nothins got him but Godbody's eyes.

I dunno how long Godbody held on to him like that, with everybody watchin. One funny thing, Melissa's face is wet, she's holdin her two hands together tight but I never hear a sound from her. After a time Godbody reaches out one big hand and begins strokin the side of Hobo's head. I never seen a man do just that, not just that way, to anythin but a horse. It was a gentlin. He kept on holdin him with the eyes, but you could see the starch go out of Wellen's shoulders and arms and he quit that fast tight breathin too. His mouth come open like a little kid does first time he sees a elephant or a grown person cryin or somethin.

Godbody's hand stops and he takes it away. Nobody says nothin for a time but Wellen is tryin, his face and mouth keeps workin. I get the crazy idea that maybe he is talkin after all but some way you can't hear. I get the crazy idea too that Godbody can hear it, because when he talks it's like he answers something: "No," he says, "it's for loving."

Then Wellen says, "It's no good."

Godbody says, "It's for loving with. It ain't for loving by. If you can do the loving with or without it—you can love with it."

Wellen says, "I don't know what you mean."

Melissa says somethin. It makes me jump. What is happenin in there has me so hung up I don't expect another voice. She says, "I know."

Godbody takes his eyes off Wellen at last, which makes him blink, and turns them on Melissa Franck. "Yeah," he says, "you do." He did not tell her to do nothin, but she went straight to Hobo and takes his hand. They go outside. I get scared they are goin to come around where I am, and I'm right, they do. It's so dark out there they can't see a damn thing, but I been out here now a long time. I can see enough so I know they're standin there, and she puts her arms around him.

He says, "What are you doing?"

She says, "You can hit me if you want to, Hobo, but you don't need to."

He has a funny voice now, half funny, half scared. "How the hell can I rip your clo'es off you're already nekkid?"

She says, "Touch me." She sits down on the ground, so does he. She lays back. "Touch me."

I don't know if he does or not. I can't see. I stick my eye back to the hole.

They're sittin around the big bowl on the floor, eatin. Godbody eats like he really digs it, both hands, mouth full, chewin quick to get more in soon. Mister Merriweather is like a squirrel, holdin himself all together tight, nibblin real fast. He says "I feel very strange. Very strange. As if I'm not here."

The preacher nodded his head. "I know what you mean, Andy." His wife said, "I don't. I'm here. I think I've spent all my life just on the way here." The preacher says, "That's it. I'm still on the way." And Mister Merriweather wags his head a lot and says, "That's it, that's it." He looks very sad at Godbody. "I don't think I can get all the way here, like you people."

"I can," says the preacher, and all of a sudden his wife kneels up and kisses him on the mouth. He says to the banker, "I don't know when. I've got a lot of unlearning to do—more than you, I think."

"Yes," says Mister Merriweather, sad, "but you're not afraid."

In the nearby dark I hear Hobo Wellen whisperin excited, "Feel that, feel it. Hard as a rock and I never hit you."

"Take off your clothes . . . "

There's a shufflin and shiftin around in the dark. He says, "I never been nekkid with a girl before."

"You're always naked," she says; she sounds like Godbody the way she talks. "Everyone always is, under their clothes."

"Oh, it feels good, up against you. Oh, it feels good."

"Yes . . . "

He says, "I'm afraid I'll hurt you with it, so big."

"Don't be afraid. Don't ever be afraid again."

He cries out, after a time, "Oh, I can't, you're too little, oh, it won't work!"

"That isn't your fault, it's mine," she says, and he cries out again, "I told you, I told you—it's going away!"

She says to him real fierce, "Now this is what Godbody meant, this is the time you have to remember what he said and believe. You have to love, Hobo. Not me, if you don't want to, but—but, well, women, a woman. Love with your penis, but if you can't, love some other way. Love with it, not by it. Now do you understand?"

"I never loved nothing or nobody," says Hobo Wellen, like he's findin somethin out for the first time. "How do you learn a thing like that?"

"I don't know," she says, "you just—do it, I guess. Hold me, Hobo. Hold me and be still."

He says "Melissa . . . "

"Yes, Hobo."

"Could I kiss you?"

"Yes, Hobo."

They got quiet again.

Inside they all got quiet. It's like they are waitin for somethin.

From the dark I hear Hobo whisperin, "It's coming back."

I am lookin at Britt Svenglund, layin across the bottom of the bed by Godbody's feet, Godbody lookin at the big candle flame, her lookin at him the same way. The Curriers are holdin hands, him in his clothes, her nekkid and shiny like she had a light inside her, happy. He's rasslin somethin in his head, you can see. And Mister Merriweather the banker hunkered down, his face hid, lookin miserable. I think I know. It's like there's more on him than he can handle.

All of a sudden I wish I could be part of it.

Melissa: "Ah! Don't stop."

Hobo: "I don't want to hurt you."

Melissa: "Don't stop!"

I wish I could be part of that, too.

She give a gasp and then a long shaky sigh, and he said, like it was tore out of him, "I . . . love . . . you," and right then they both give a real quiet shout, that's the only way to say it, and they did it again.

And Mister Merriweather the banker was on his feet lookin around, and I never seen such a face in all my life. I had to think it was because he hears the two outside but it isn't that, it's something much bigger. It was like he was a man standin all alone top of a mountain and he seen somethin —somebody standin in the valley so tall he got to look up.

That dried-up, cold-blooded little bastard was somehow on fire, how the hell do you say somethin when it ain't like nothin you ever seen before?

Mr. Currier, he's scared, he yells, "Andy! Are you all right?" and right away Godbody is kneelin by him, put his hands on him, "Let him be. Let him be. I seen the like before. He's Godstruck."

Mr. Currier sits back, watchin the banker. Godbody goes back to the bed. Mister Merriweather is lookin up, lookin through the roof, lookin through the sky I'll swear. The waitin feeling starts to grow and grow. I am like paralyzed. Somethin's comin at me through those walls like when you open a furnace door, but it ain't heat.

Around the side I hear Melissa Franck, it's like singin: "I thought I could never do it!" and Hobo, "Me too, me too!" "Come on," she says.

So I know it ain't just me, because when they show up at the door, the both of them nekkid and with an arm around each other and smilin, they stop sudden at the sight of the man standin there swayin, and they creep in quiet and kneel down with the others. And Mister Merriweather begins to speak in a great big brand new voice:

"This is the answer!

"The answer is not in getting and keeping, but in getting and giving.

"The answer is not in saving and preserving, but in growing and changing.

"The answer is not in making things stop, but in making things go.

"The answer is not in covering and hiding, but in touching and sharing.

"The answer is not in thinking, but in feeling.

"The answer is not death, but love.

"Not death, but life.

"Not death!"

And then that man sang a note. It was a great big Ahhhh, on and on, louder and louder, he held up his arms and that note come from him in a voice so much bigger'n him you couldn't believe it. And I knew what it was: it was all the things he said wasn't all he had to say, all the rest he had to say there was no words for but it had to be said and it come out in that great big sound he made, holdin up his arms and turnin and turnin; oh, it went on too long for it to be really him, somethin was singin that note through him, it wasn't him at all.

And he went to Godbody who jumped up eager and he kissed Godbody on the mouth, and he turned to Britt Svenglund and he put his arms around her and he kissed her on the mouth, and then he kissed Hobo Wellen, and Hobo hugged him close and willin, and he kissed Melissa Franck and Dan Currier and each one he touched seemed somehow to light up and the tears was streamin out of their eyes and I'm only a goddam pissant part-time cop but I'm here to tell you that I will never live so long I'll stop regretting I was not there in that room to have that man kiss me, and you can think what you like. And the last one he went to was Liza Currier and she put out her arms and came to him laughin, and at that very moment somebody grabbed hard at my shoulder and tipped me away from the house wall and a hard hand goes down to my hip and snatches out my police special and I fall back and look up and there standin over me flooded with light from the open window is Mrs. Mayhew, her face twisted up like somethin straight out of hell.

She is lookin in at nekkid Liza Currier flyin to the open arms of Mister Merriweather, and she don't give a damn if they can see her and she says with spit flyin out of her mouth, "That rotten little bitch I'll kill her," and she points my gun and pulls the trigger. And I am up off the ground and grab her wrist with my left and let her have a punch alongside the jaw I swear spins her around twice before she hits the ground outside in the dark, and then I'm in through the window, the whole thing happenin so fast it's like the gun was goin off and everythin went on durin the one bang.

There was blue sneezy smoke and Mister Merriweather holdin Liza Currier in his arms, and between them and me big nekkid Godbody with a little hole in his chest. He smiles at me and turns around and in the middle of his back is another hole you could put almost your fist in. Still turnin he goes down like a tall tree.

Oh, there is a terrible scream, the one scream from Liza and Britt and Melissa, a scream so big it taken three throats to make it. And from the three men come a growl I hope never to hear again because, but for a miracle, it's the last thing a man is likely to hear. I got my miracle. But for Godbody them three would have tore me in pieces like wolves.

Godbody cries, "Stop."

Already the women have him to the low bed, already tryin that useless dabbin of the blood. "It ain't him," Godbody says. "It was a woman out there."

"Mrs. Mayhew," Melissa says like spittin.

Godbody said, "This guy tried to stop her. Who are you?"

"Harry Salz."

He got a funny small smile. "I guess you are, but you can do better." The smile went away fast. This guy hurt. One of the women started to cry. Godbody said a very strange thing then, he said, "It's always like this. Usually not so soon, though." He untwisted his face and looked at everybody gathered around. He raised up his head and kind of clumsy pushed aside the cloth Britt was holdin on his chest.

He looked at the hole. Blood filled and emptied in it, filled and emptied. "This really is a hell of a way to make a living," says Godbody, and his eyes close.

I think we all stop breathin just then, but he opens his eyes again and looks all around again. The way his eyes are I think we must look kind of misty to him by then. His voice is goin into a fog too when he talks. "Are you of a mind to listen to me?" He did not need any answer to that. "Then when that Mrs. Mayhew comes in, don't hassle her." He could still smile a little. "I know what you're thinking, Dan: 'Forgive them, they know not what they do.' It's sort of like that, she don't know what she's doing, but I want you to know it's God's work. Yeah.

"What I want, what I really want you to do is what she says long as she's here. Later maybe, play it by ear, but for now, yes Mrs. Mayhew, no Mrs. Mayhew, you're right Mrs. Mayhew, no matter what she says or does. You hear? No matter what. If you can do that everything is cool."

He closes his eyes again and again nobody breathes. Then he says, "Try to remember me. If you're goin to tell what I said, make it what I said and not what somebody thinks I said or what somebody wishes I'd said. Also don't anybody forget I sweat and stink sometimes, and some people-stinks are better'n all the roses in the world. Also I talk people-talk and try to keep things simple. I got no rules to recite except love each other; God, if you'd all only do that, you wouldn't need no other rules at all, not one.

"Outdoors naked is all the cathedrals I ever want in my name, all the robes and collars as well. Straight, simple, honest talk is all the services anybody ever needs to hold for me, and if you work out a form for it I won't come.

"If ever you want to touch the hand and the heart of God Almighty, you can do it through the body of someone you love. Anytime. Anywhere. Without no middleman.

"I'll see you around." He died.

She come in while we was all cryin. Yes, me too. I don't want to talk about it. We said yes Mrs. Mayhew and the rest. She made it plain she had us each and every one by the balls. She made it plain she was goin to cover for us, her and Mister Merriweather who would now do what she said. We knew damn well she would cover for us because if she blew the whistle we would all be taken away from her one way or the other. Once she was satisfied Godbody was a stranger around here she give us our orders, get rid of him. Get rid of "it" is what she said. Britt has enough acres of hillside and rocks, she could find where. She took me aside and told me to remember.

We said yes Mrs. Mayhew, and she left us alone with our dead. She took the Currier's car.

That was Friday.

Sunday

ELEVEN O'CLOCK WORSHIP Service proceeded neatly and decorously as usual, with the usual amount of unusual. There were always strangers, up from the city, often a backslider returned (would it be just once?) and occasionally a hopeless secularite, suddenly and astonishingly appearing in the pews. This particular Sunday the usual unusual was supplied by Hobart Wellen, shined and pressed, accompanied by surely the town's least brazen hussy, Melissa Franck. To the truly discerning student of the unusual, one would have to add the special size and shine of three pairs of eyes: those of Britt Svenglund (paying one of her rare visits), Liza Currier and the aforementioned Melissa. The brightness of tears, perhaps, or love newly found, or of foreknowledge. Who could possibly imagine that it might be all three at once? Then there were the two kinds of righteousness displayed by Mr. Merriweather and Mrs. Mayhew (appearing as usual in one of her capital-H Hats) and the really astonishing phenomenon of Mrs. Merriweather, usually a grey-on-grey (with dog hairs) composition but today, looking fifteen years younger and smiling all the time, wearing bright yellow and some real flowers in her hair. (One of the things she was smiling about was a Mrs. Holloway's reaction to her response about Boo.) "And how is dear Boo?" Mrs. Holloway, who gossiped about Boo, had asked mischievously, and little Mrs. Merriweather had answered, "Very happy, thank you. We put him in the kennels yesterday, out to stud."

Hymn and collect, creed and hymn, neat and orderly. Who noticed the firm closed lips of the minister during the I believe? Later, there would be many who said they did. As a matter of strict truth, there were quite a few who sat through even this sermon nodding gently, with small benign smiles on their faces, who did not hear a word and who worked up their passionate opinions on the whole matter only after Wednesday's paper came out.

Here is the sermon as delivered by Dr. Daniel Currier.

Goodbye.

A long pause—so long that feet began to shift audibly. Dr. Currier stood on the pulpit (which always seemed so small for him) with his elbows resting comfortably on the lectern and waited until the balance between waning interest and waxing irritation suited him.

"Goodbye" is a word, a little clumping of words, which means God be with you. I mean this for you all with all my heart.

You must know that I am not, I have tried very hard not to be, the biblical scholar out to make biblical scholars of his congregation, making himself obscure with true Aramaic and Greek pronunciations. Yet I shall confess to you that for nearly thirty hours yesterday and this morning I have been locked up with my books, playing the scholar.

I have discovered some extraordinary things. The most extraordinary thing of all is that I did not have to go near the extraordinary part of my reference shelf. Anyone can find what I have found—what has changed my life and the lives of some very dear friends, and what may well make a drastic upheaval in some of yours—with nothing but a Bible, a concordance and any fairly competent history of Christianity. Let me tell you what I have found.

We are Christians—that is to say, worshippers of the Christ Jesus of Nazareth, in Whose name we have established this sanctuary and all the forms, written and unwritten, which go forth in it.

From Sunday to Sunday, it seems there is a comforting sameness to this house of worship and its services, the way they are conducted, and the way we behave on either side of the altar rail. Yet there have been changes. A perfect example is this: The careful and modest clothes worn by you ladies here today would have been unacceptable not only in the church, but on the beach, within the living memory of some of our senior parishioners. Right, Mr. Malcolm? Miss Schutz?

Miss Schutz, aged 84, had been fast asleep since the second hymn, but old Malcolm nodded vigorously and scanned the ladies· about him with rather more gusto than they liked.

We are using a modern-English Bible, and many of our hymns are new or have been rearranged. There will certainly be further changes. Whether we like that or not, we can regard the idea soberly because they have not happened yet. We know there have been changes, too, but it seems a little harder to understand that changes in Christian worship did not begin twenty years ago, or fifty, or at the moment Martin Luther nailed his manuscript to a church door hundreds of years ago. The real changes began with the death of the last of the disciples—the men who actually talked with Jesus and were taught by Him.

We liked to lull ourselves with the idea that changes are all to the good—that what we have is an improvement on what we had. Well, in some ways that is so. For all their quarrels and disagreements, the Christian churches have millions of supporters and own billions of dollars worth of real property. If that is an improvement over what the Apostles had, then sobeit.

But is it an improvement in Christianity, as Christ saw it and taught it?

What was the early worship like?

There is one really fascinating way to find out. All through church history you can find references to councils, called for the purpose of setting forth church doctrine and church practices. In announcing that thus-and-so should henceforth be done, they also announced what should *not* be done.

And that's the important point. You do not forbid something unless people are doing it.

Through a study of what these councils have forbidden, we know what Christians were doing at the time. Where Christianity was changed, it was changed gradually, and this kind of study shows us step by step how these changes were brought about—and why. You see, what I am getting to is not what changes have been made, but what Christianity was before it was changed.

Let me tell you now, without documenting all the steps with dates and place—but mind you, that can be done—just what the worship of God through Christ was as it was left to us by Jesus of Nazareth and his disciples.

There was no house of worship. Sometimes by choice, often to hide from persecution, the worshippers met at some quiet, secret place.

There was no officiating priest.

There were no distinctions as to race or age, wealth or poverty or sex. The greatest appeal of Christianity, as a matter of fact, was to the masses, the slaves, and women, all of whom were accepted equally. It is interesting to note here that in our church, ordination of women has occurred only within the past fifteen years, and less than half of one-percent of our ministers are women.

There was the "kiss of peace." On gathering, each person embraced every other.

There was a feast—it was called *Agape*. It was a real meal.

Afterward, the people sat together in an aura of love

and replenishment, and awaited theolepsy—a word which means "seized of God." You have heard of—laughed at—people who "speak in tongues," who work themselves up into religious frenzies, who fall into fits or wild dances. This seems far removed from our decent modern practices—yet it was precisely this which the apostolic Church courted and welcomed. It is said over and over in Scripture and in commentaries that this was a real and definite experience, and that once a person had experienced it, he was forever changed. Even to be in the presence of this experience, when it happened to another person, is said to have been an unforgettable adventure, and one which one would seek out again for the rest of one's life. It is this which enabled the Christians in the Roman era to march into the arena smiling and singing and thanking God as they were stabbed and burned and torn to pieces by wild animals . . . A fascinating aside on this—the word "thank" in English derives from the same root as the word "think." These people could do what they did, not through sheer courage, but because they were "thinking God"—reliving the theoleptic experience . . .

With this picture in mind of an early Christian worship service, watch what happened:

First the Eucharist—the bread and wine symbolizing the body and blood of Christ—was introduced into the Agape, the love feast. Then came the ruling that an Agape could not be held unless a bishop were present to bless the food. Next came the order that the bishop was to remain apart and standing—above—the celebrants. Then it was ordained that instead of kissing one another, everyone had to kiss the priest, and later still, a piece of wood which was handed around and passed to him. Then the kiss was abolished altogether, and in 363 the Council of Laodicea forbade the celebration of the Agape inside the churches, at which point it was forever separated from the Eucharist. Finally it disappeared altogether. One writer has remarked that champagne at a wedding, and port wine at a funeral, are all that is left of fundamental Christian worship!

This is not strictly true. Our good friends the Quakers have something remaining of it, when without a priest they sit at meeting and await the holy urge to speak. Even that, however, is a far cry from the early worship practiced by the people who actually knew Jesus.

You have a right to ask why—why were these changes made? For they were made by men, not God, out of their own inventiveness, and not by Scripture. Most of these changes came about in the third and fourth centuries after Christ died. And mind you, these were not three or four modern centuries, with widespread reading and printing and great libraries and archives to consult: these were primitive centuries when events of five or ten years back must have seemed like remote myths and were subject to dilution from every word-of-mouth transmission. One might say recklessly that modern Christian worship was born, not in Galilee and on the Mount and Golgotha, but hundreds of years later by remote strangers.

Again: why? I will tell you why, but I will warn you that the discovery chilled my blood.

When we take up our collection in this sanctuary, what happens? The ushers pass the salvers, collect them, and bring them to me. I take them, *turn my back on you,* and hold them up to the altar. Fix on that—take a snapshot of that. Use it as a symbol of what we do here when we practice worship. Let the offering represent worship. You give of this substance and it is collected and brought to me. Only through me does it reach the altar, or God. This is what a minister, pastor, priest has become—a channel so that only through channels can the congregation reach God.

And why did these stepfathers of the early church want this?

This is the chilling answer: so they could eliminate theolepsy—the direct contact between man and God.

And why eliminate that?

Because, my friends, this is the only way possible for the organized church to make a buck.

I hope you'll forgive the vulgarity in this holy place, but it is the truth. Unless the church stamped out real religious experience, it could not control the worldly aspects of church organization—money and power, which, as I'm sure you know, the church has sought and found for two thousand years . . .

I must say a word about prayer here. It is seldom, indeed, that anyone can reach a religious rapture by praying alone. Theolepsy seems to be a group experience—something about the presence of a group seems to bring it about in the God-struck individual . . .

Not ten years ago there was a sudden resurgence of "speaking in tongues" in the Episcopal church, and it was firmly put down. It always is—it always will be in any church of any size.

I see some of you looking uncomfortable. Let me show you this paper before you begin to think in terms of complaining to the District or to my superiors about what I have said here today. This is a carbon copy of my resignation, effective as of noon today—when I walk through these doors. I shall leave it here on the lectern for your examination.

From the sanctuary: gasps, and a hiss of whispering.

I shall sum up now. Please hear me out.

I have dedicated the most important part of my life to the understanding of the teachings of Jesus, and my efforts have been equally dedicated to passing these on to others. I have now come to a point where I feel that I am in the wrong place. The wrong place is a place which by its very nature prohibits—worship. The wrong place is a place which takes the prime teaching of the Man of Nazareth—that he voluntarily relieved us of sin and therefore of guilt—and has turned it into the most efficient guilt-factory ever known on this planet. It was Paul —who, by the way, never knew Jesus—who put the onus on sex, not Jesus; and it was a whole series of his successors who set up controls on the two most powerful motivations we have—to procreate and to worship. I want my God for my pastor, not my bishop nor any other man. I want to love without shame and to worship without dilution; and feeling so, my friends, I feel myself disqualified for this job.

In closing and farewell, let me follow precedent by giving you texts, with chapter and verse:

Acts, 7:48 and 9: Howbeit, the most high dwelleth not in a temple made with hands . . . Heaven is my throne, and earth my footstool; what house will ye build me? saith the Lord. First Corinthians, 20: Therefore glorify God in your body, and in your spirit, which are God's. You'll say I took that out of context, and you're right. Matthew, 6: 5: But thou, when thou prayest, thou shalt not be as the hypocrites are . . . standing . . . in the corners of the streets, that they may be seen of men. But thou, when thou prayest, enter into thy closet, and shut the door, pray to thy father which is in secret, and thy father which seeth in secret shall reward thee openly.

God be with you all, which is to say—
Goodbye.

They filed out: this was the time of greeting, of shaking hands. Daniel Currier stood just outside the door as two lines, not one, pushed past—the one shouldering out, angry, haughty, bewildered, frightened; the other stopping to speak to him: can't mean it, good for you, waited years to hear the like, discredit to your church, your town, your profession and your God, what about the Tuesday tea?

Want my check back from the Building Fund. "There's more to this than meets the eye; *I* know where the body is buried." (Thank you, Mrs. Mayhew; a nice figure of speech.)

And about one in five said to him softly, "Dan, where are you going? Because wherever you go with that kind of talk, I want to be there too." These he sent to the oak tree at the corner of the parking lot to wait for him.

It was over at last, and the reaction set in: joy, release, fatigue, and the deepest desire to be naked with Liza in his arms. He told her this, and she closed her eyes and turned up her face to be kissed. Then hand-in-hand they went to the oak tree, followed by the glares, the frightened glances, the envious stares, the tittering, the grumblings, the whispers of the people. Awaiting him was a small crowd: Wellen and Melissa, the Merriweathers, Harry Salz the policeman, and Britt Svenglund looking lovely in an unadorned but beautifully draped long gown of forest-green jersey. Along with them were some friends and some strangers: a man with a blind girl who said to him heartily, "Rev, I'd follow you to hell even if you were wrong, and I think you're right," and two schoolteacherish types and a thin young man with a pipe who kept saying, "Wow. Oh, wow." All in all, twenty-odd.

He hadn't meant to address them all, but he had to; they fell silent when he began to speak to the hearty man. He said, "I don't want to lead anyone. That's for pastors— shepherds—and I've had my fill of sheep. This afternoon I am going to the mountain with some friends and pay my respects to someone I love. If you'd like to be there, you're welcome, but do not follow me because I will not lead."

They wanted to know where, and Britt told them, and Liza told them that if they knew of anyone else who felt as they did, bring them along. "Three o'clock."

It was half-past noon by then, and the Curriers hurried

to the parsonage as they usually did for Sunday dinner. Someone had thrown half a brick through the front-door glass, and on the floor were two papers slipped under the door. Dan Currier picked them up and looked at them and laughed like a trumpet, for one said, "God bless you," and the other, "God have mercy on you." He locked the inner door and they never even bothered with the kitchen but crossed the living room, where the boxes full of personal linens and books were piled, and went upstairs. Someone knocked and they ignored it. The phone rang and Liza knocked it off its cradle in passing, using her elbow because with both hands she was unbuttoning the brown-and-yellow dress. The bedroom was awash with sun, more than ever before with the drapes down. Liza was out of all her clothes before Dan had his jacket off.

"When we get where we're going," he said, "I won't wear clothes at all, but if I have to, they're going to be clothes that can come off faster than yours."

"You'd look cute in my brown-and-yellow dress."

"Seriously," he said, "there's a lot of sense in unisex clothes. I've read all sorts of horrified comment about them, how they're trying to homogenize the sexes. I don't think that's so. I think that you and I dressed in identical clothes—clothes that fit, idiot—could be spotted unmistakably as a man and a woman at two hundred yards, even if we had the same length hair."

"I think you're right," she said. "*Do* hurry . . . Dan, d'you suppose manly men's clothes and girly girl clothes are really for people who aren't sure what sex they belong to?"

"I do believe you're right!" He flung himself down beside her. "Anyway, I know what sex you belong to."

"Really, sir? Which?"

"Me," he said, and suddenly the bantering and the chatter were gone and he knelt up and bent over her. He rubbed his cheek and hair over her body, he flung her legs wide and pressed his face into the scant fine hair between them. She smelt clean and animal and female and good; he tasted her, mildly salt-bitter at first and then sweet and smooth. He moved back and looked at her vulva, the brown-pink-rosy folds of it, neat, ingenious, welcoming. "Oh God," she cried, "I love your eyes on me, your hands."

"I love you," he said. "I love you so much."

"And so well," she crooned as he brought his weight on her. He smoothed her hair away from her face and kissed and kissed her while they made calm and knowing adjustments, each to the other, and his penis slid in gently, untouched by hands. "Do you suppose . . . he can see us?"

"I hope so," he said into her warm neck. They gave themselves up to each other, sunlit, glad.

But the subject was still there afterward, when, spent, he rolled away and lay on his back. She touched his stomach and said, "Nobody, not even Godbody, could tell if this is your sweat or mine," and all of a sudden the salt stung his eyes and, seeing it, she began to cry too. "It didn't have to happen," she wept, "it didn't."

Oddly enough, that stopped his tears, and something greater than grief moved within him. "Maybe it did," he said.

Three o'clock, and the hillside dotted with people, about fifty by now, a camera or two, even a ferret-faced girl with a tape recorder. Just what word had gotten around was hard to say, but there was an air of windblown excitement, a feeling of something impending. Dan Currier, walking up the slope past the ledge on which stood Britt Svenglund's house, found himself liking the looks of most of these people. There were a lot of hard hands around, and women fit for breeding and compassion and being close, not distant, when things were bad; children with early tans and the bloom of winter windburn under it, and lovers looking newly at the world tinted the other lover's colors. A God-body kind of crowd, he thought, and Liza beside him turned and smiled into his eyes, doubtless with the same thought. It could have been no other.

Then, screams.

Currier raced up over the rocky slope and into the woods. In the shadowed green he caught a flicker of a green more luminescent: Britt Svenglund's long gown, held high as she bounded down the hill. "Britt!" he called. "Over here!" He stopped, partly to be sure she saw him and partly to wait for Liza, whom he had far outdistanced. She came up panting.

"Dan—what is it?"

"Britt. Oh, there's Melissa too."

"Why did they go up *there?*"

They exchanged a startled look and then turned again up hill, leaping and scrambling. Britt and Melissa, having seen them, turned and went back up, which meant yes, that's where they were going.

Winded, they reached the high glade and stopped.

Across a small clearing was a sheer rock wall, and its secret was raped. Here was a small deep cave, here they had carried a burden and wept, and then Currier and Wellen, Merriweather and the policeman had pried the rubble away from a huge boulder a little upslope from the cave mouth, had carried rocks downhill from it, had used a two-man tree trunk as a lever and had started the boulder moving, where with their rocks for guides it had rolled down and planted itself solidly in the cave-mouth.

It had rolled away again—uphill.

Britt and Melissa stood terrified, holding each other.

"Britt—"

"He is gone," she said. She wept. "Oh, I might have seen him once more, even like that, but I wasn't here, I wasn't here."

Melissa stroked her long hair. Currier demanded, "Who moved the rock?"

"Nobody could move that rock," Liza said.

They approached the cave, bent and crowded in. It was empty.

Outside, they heard the noise of people approaching.

Currier, suddenly, released a great boom of laughter that flung itself about the echoing rock. "I can tell them now. Don't you see? It doesn't have to be our secret."

"Corpus delicti," said Liza, and suddenly she too laughed wildly. Britt looked at her, almost horrified. Liza hugged her and kissed her cheek. "Oh darling, I'm sorry," she cried, "but I couldn't help it. Mrs. Mayhew came up to us after service and reminded us that she knew where the body was buried."

"She can't have us now," said Dan Currier, and went out to meet the people, to talk about God the pastor and how He could be touched through the body, and how the currents of life could save life, and how to thwart those who wanted to stop.

. . . While down on Britt's ledge the blind girl waited for her father to come back. She heard a step, not his, and a voice. "What's your name?"

She told him and suddenly felt the hard smoothness of his wrists against the sides of her neck. "Well, so you are," he said, and then, ingenuously, "Listen, you don't like being blind, do you?"

"Like it?"

"Well, I thought I'd ask. Some people do. Here, I'll fix it for you."

He put his hands on her face. They were enormous. The

fingertips probed gently and the hands slid over her eyes. She heard him murmur, "Now . . . " and there came a pressure, increasing not quite enough to hurt, and then held steadily. "Now . . . " he murmured again, and something indescribable happened in her sockets and behind them, and also at the base of her brain—not quite a fever, not exactly a headache. Suddenly a very new thing began to happen to her—not possible to describe to anyone the feelings of a lifelong sightless person having the experience called "pink."

"Keep your hands over your eyes for a while," he told her cheerfully, "because the light's awful bright at first. Then when you get used to light, you'll have to teach those pretty eyes how to work."

"But they said I—"

"They said wrong. They didn't know me."

"Oh! Oh! . . . " She still could not believe it, but she would. "What's your name?"

"Godbody."

"Godbody, don't go away. Please don't."

"I got to. Got another job to do, and it's a long way. But —you'll be seeing me."

She heard his light long-paced footsteps striding away. "I'll be seeing you?" she whispered, "Be *seeing* you?"

She held on to a sapling and waited, wondering aloud, "Who is Godbody?"

AFTERWORD

BY STEPHEN DONALDSON

I GREW UP IN India, lived there through my high school years; my father was a medical missionary. As what some people called a "mish-kid," I had access to an extremely erratic supply of books. So I read whatever I could get my hands on: the Hardy boys and Paul Tillich; Dave Dawson, "WW II Fighting Ace," who singlehandedly won every air battle of the war; Agatha Christie; Bomba the Jungle Boy and Leon Uris. By the time I graduated, I got my hands on exactly three sf novels. I remember each of them distinctly, in part because they were so different from the rest of my reading, and in part because they were excellent. They were: A. J. Budrys' *Rogue Moon;* Alfred Bester's *The Stars My Destination;* and Theodore Sturgeon's *More Than Human.*

Of those three, in my case *More Than Human* represented by far the most improbable triumph of communication, the most dramatic outreach of imagination from one mind to another across the barriers of language, culture, and ideology. Of those three books, *More Than Human* is much the most down-to-earth. For that reason, it deals the most directly with issues of morality and religion. The other two were safer because they were so much further removed from my personal life.

Whatever the qualities of my imagination at that age, I was intellectually narrow-minded, religiously fundamentalist, socially protected, culturally conservative. And yet Sturgeon *came through.* Somehow he contrived to thrill me with his notion of gestalt humanity—an idea that challenged all my preconceptions about identity and ethics, about the responsibilities of relationships. *Rogue Moon* may be intellectually tougher; *The Stars My Destination* a more bravura performance. But against all the odds *More Than Human* hit me where I lived.

Under the circumstances, it was a good thing I didn't read "Microcosmic God" until later in life, when I was better able to handle its implications. Imagine a mish-kid trying to explain to his parents the concept of being responsible for God.

I mention all this because I consider this capacity to *come through* against the odds to be one of the special elements of Sturgeon's particular genius. And because it happened to me again in *Godbody.*

By most normal standards, I'm the last writer in America who ought to be asked to comment on this book. I'm disqualified by personality, preconception, and conviction. Despite all my "liberal" attitudes, I'm a closet Puritan where sex is concerned. My knee-jerk reaction to nudists is that they are out of their minds, like mothers who wrap their kids in aluminum foil to protect them from Martian rays. And I believe that the whole notion of *Godbody* (sex is the highest form of religion) is palpable nonsense. When I was offered the manuscript, I squirmed inside. I already knew I was going to hate it.

But I read it anyway, because I've read enough Sturgeon

to realize that my personality, preconceptions, and convictions were irrelevant: he could reach me if I gave him the chance. And the result is another improbable triumph of communication.

More a meditation than a novel, *Godbody* lacks most of the usual apparatus of fiction. Superficially, it is little more than an interlocking series of character sketches, culminating in tragedy and affirmation: God is love; and the tragedy is that we make a distinction between love and sex; and the affirmation is that sex *can be* love, the purest expression of God. But the book is by no means superficial. Precisely because it is so specific, so rooted in particular characters who react and speak and need in such particular ways, it becomes as profound as the word "meditation" suggests: an aching and immediate occasion for thought.

Somehow, *Godbody* overcomes all the intervening personal, cultural, and theological hinderances. It *comes through.*

Sturgeon, Theodore
Godbody

DATE			

© THE BAKER & TAYLOR CO.